The Rock:
The Beginning

by
Patrick Timm

Strategic Book Publishing and Rights Co.

Strategic Book Publishing and Rights Co.
12620 FM 1960, Suite A4-507
Houston, TX 77065
www.sbpra.com

ISBN: 978-1-61204-662-4

Design: Dedicated Book Services, Inc. (www.netdbs.com)

Acknowledgments

There are hundreds of people that helped support this project from the beginning to the very end. So if you feel like I left you out, you gotta know that there were several people who, also was probably skipped over, and for that I apologize.

My mother was a large source of support and doing some leg work for "reminding" me of locations around town.

Everyone on board the HMJ who supported me by reading the pages before I could even finish them: Nubwicki, Contreras, Jazz, Tapp, JPud, Marcus. LBJ and Garrard for their inspiration for what to do for several large portions of the book, while sitting by the ladders.

The people on land who read it as soon as it was done and could wait to finish it because it was so addicting, including Mo, Slash, Saraha, Sarah, Cheryl, Stewart, and several others I can't begin to list.

Although, not part of the book the core group of friends who got me through a very rough patch and helped me right the ship.

Finally, as many people would suspect, the woman who drove me to start this book, by being the wonderful person she was.

The Rock
The Beginning
by Patrick Timm

Introduction

My name is Logan. Before I begin, I should provide a little bit of my life before the disease reached the US. I was born to two loving parents about twenty years before it happened. By the sixth year, my father had bounced from job to job to the bottle, and by the eighth, he was gone, out of my life. To this day I have no idea where he disappeared to.

My mom raised me and my little sister on her own while teaching Monday to Friday and waitressing on weekends. I was a typical teenager before all this happened, I had a part-time job myself, working at a local grocery store and going to community college. I drank and smoked — a typical rebellious teen. The day I heard about the disease hitting China, I remember thinking "'Bout time they thinned the mob." But then the disease popped up in Africa and Europe.

Our overseas forces were pulled from their duties and whatnot, and all reserve forces were called up to the coasts and southern borders. The navy deployed along the coast to prevent ships from reaching us, and for awhile it all seemed to be effective. All everyone was talking about was the disease and how it was incurable. College classes, office buildings, and even stores were closed. Churches were crammed wall to wall with people. You'd hear rumors about riots, but the media was blacked out. The president and generals gave speeches saying how it would never reach the US, and then the government stepped up its forces on the borders when the rest of the world was desperately trying to get in. The draft was reinstituted, but instead of boot camp, boys were given rifles and told to go here or there. Sometimes they weren't even given uniforms. That's when I realized everything was falling apart.

The Rock Island Arsenal had been the major employer for something like eighty years, and suddenly it became quiet. No one entered and no one left. There was just a letter to the non-military personnel that their services were no longer needed. That's when I go the phone call that probably saved my life. It was the army recruiter saying my number was called. Luckily I was slick-tongued and gave him some sob story about a sick grandma. He said to report to the Rock within the next week. I said my goodbyes. Shit was about to hit the proverbial fan. The Rock was a perfect fort in terms of defending it, there were three bridges leading onto the island. The one bridge that connected the Rock to Iowa was an old fashioned swing bridge.

When I arrived, I was sent to a small building where twenty other local guys were getting uniforms. They told us we were to have no contact with the outside world. *What the Fuck?* I thought. Then they took us to a theater, and once I was seated I figured my life as I knew it was over—even though I had no idea what I was in for.

Then a big screen came alive with images of the disease from all over the world. Then it showed how to stop it. Just like in those Hollywood movies, a mighty blow to the head would do it.

Our mission was to protect the Rock, which had become some sort of mega-armory almost overnight. Workers worked twelve hours a day to protect our country. I was issued my M16 and a set of fatigues that were a little too tight. I was partnered with Tommy Briggs, who was from a farming town upriver. Our squad was to patrol the worst corner in the sector, where there was a big old field and nothing else. If you stood in one spot, you could see our entire area. It was so lame, but looking back on it, I miss those days.

One day we were all called into the theater. The isolation strategy was failing everywhere. The disease had reached LA, NYC and the Florida panhandle. A was contained, but NYC and the Southeast were to be evacuated but we were to stay put. The Army Corps of Engineers was building a super fence line in the Great Plains. More workers were brought onto the island, as well as about 400 semis full of food and supplies. At first it was a trickle, but more and more people began to head west to help build this super-fort, while we started a fence line around the island. "Why do we need a fence? I thought the Rock was safe," was what all the local kids were wondering.

I thought of my family and wished I could get a hold of them. My day finally came; in "orderly" fashion we were allowed a thirty-minute phone call. I called my mom, and she picked up after two rings. Because she had no money, she was staying with my sister. My heart sank as I begged her to head for the West. She was stubborn because news of the impending danger had barely reached them. After a gut wrenching thirty minutes, I said my final goodbyes. Tommy also called his dad—they too were staying. That was the last time I saw him, and the rumor mill said he was shot trying to escape. *Escape? What are we, prisoners?* I thought.

News began to trickle that it had reached Chicago. All three bridges were closed; the two east bridges were blocked off by a dozen or so cars. The west bridge was rotated so that nothing could get through. The workers were the first to protest their imprisonment, in mass they swam ashore and presumably headed west. We were under manned was an understatement. I worked twenty hours a day guarding about a hundred workers making ammo for guns that soon couldn't fire them. That's when acting base commander Col. Majors said, "We'll open the two east bridges. Anyone wanting off has three hours to leave."

He took the Rock's four helicopters and told everyone in the rest of the area about the bridge openings. About twenty people left the Rock and close to 500 people joined the island. As an original member, I was promoted to corporal and tasked with training new guards.

Of the 500, about 400 were poor women and children. The island still had its two original doctors and four nurses to care for almost 700 people. The newbies were processed in, and women and children were assigned tasks like preparing the golf course for farming. Everyone was expected to carry their weight.

I was promoted again, this time to squad leader. I was the backup if something happened to the patrols, which were now comprised of four men. I got a sweet Humvee and a new .50 caliber machine gun. I looked at the list of names just processed, but my mom's wasn't there. I felt a tear run down my cheek. I wiped it away and looked at the list, but didn't recognize any names.

By now we'd been on the island for six months and were well prepared for the inevitable. At each of the three entrances to the Rock were three Humvees, sixteen men with M16s, and a heavy gate. The island perimeter was divided into sixteen areas, each with four to six guards at any given time, plus three squad leaders roving the island and one shift commander. Shifts were a piece of cake—twelve hours on, twelve hours as backup, and then twelve hours of free time. Life was good those first three weeks, before the winds started to shift.

I was just sitting down to eat when there was a massive blinding explosion to the north. It was the nuclear power plant, and I wouldn't see the sun for almost six months. Fires raged everywhere to the north. The air was smoky and hard to breathe. The backup diesel generator kicked in, and we went on emergency conservation mode. According to the engineer, we had enough fuel for probably a year or so.

Two days later, the guards at the north gate spotted a figure stagger toward the gate. One of the guards ordered the figure to stop over the public address, but he kept plodding toward the gate. He'd just reached the gate as I arrived. Still no response, so I gave the order. The first shot hit him in the stomach, and the leader at the gate yelled in horror as the round had no effect. *The disease had reached the Rock.*

I remembered my "training," where they'd said something about blunt trauma to the head. So I calmed the gate leader and the others. One of the machine gunners opened fire and turned the creature into goo. I reported to the shift commander, Lt. Jon Greene, a Bible thumper who'd said this was God's punishment and had let his chain of command know. After shift we were all debriefed. Three hours later we heard over the PA the *Star Spangled Banner*, followed by an announcement from Col. Majors. "Can I have all of your attention? This is Col. Majors. We've had our first encounter with the disease. Everyone remain calm, please. The Rock is designed to protect us. The only way we can outlast them is to continue to do what we're doing. Be vigilant, keep doing your duty, and we will prevail. Nothing can conquer us as long as we work together. God bless all of you and the rest of humanity." It was quiet for about three days after that, although without the sun it was hard to define a day.

"Is that a man, or is it one of *them*?" was frequently asked question. Of course the word "zombie" was used—and these were real zombies, not a Hollywood creation. On the third day, I had just laid down when I heard the unmistakable sound of gunfire. I dressed quickly and waited for an announcement. As I left my house, I heard, "Medical personnel report to Sector Five" come over the PA.

When I went on shift ten hours later, I found out that the patrol from Sector Five had strayed into Sector Six, and the guys in six were trigger happy and mowed them down. Now, we'd had gun training and were given call signs—you'd yell "thunder" if you saw movement. The proper response was "flash." You'd repeat it once, and if you got no response you'd fire a shot toward the movement. Most would just yell any old thing, which worked fine because the zombies didn't speak.

The next shift was the beginning of the fun times. We were still getting three meals, but they were becoming less and less filling. I relieved a guy named Chuck. I could never pronounce his last name, but that didn't matter then. But Chuck loved two things playing with fire and practical jokes. About seven hours into my shift, I heard over the radio, "Contact. Approximately twenty at Sector Three." I patrolled Zone A, and since Sector Three was in Zone C, I had to race across the island. I could hear people in Sector Three yelling frantically, begging for more ammo and help. There was too many of them. When I reached the gate, I could see why they were scared. It was an endless mob of those creatures. That's when I heard the distinctive noise of a helicopter overhead, followed by the sound of rockets whizzing by. Cheers rang out, but they were short-lived. The airborne ash had clogged the copter's engine intake, and the crew's screams could be heard via the various radios as it went down. By this time, the reserve backup forces had arrived, and the remaining zombies were squashed.

The next morning began with the inventory officer—some bitch who'd slept her way to that job—announcing over the PA that "due to last night's waste of ammo, all units will have half the allotted ammo as normal." No one was pleased, and a few squad leaders talked of rioting. But that quickly faded when news finally came from the super-fort. The Director of Homeland Security was in charge because the president and most of his cabinet and senior military personnel were MIA—presumed either dead or undead when communication with their "secure" location was lost. Now "President" Stevens, former Director of Homeland of Security, stated in his speech that zombies had reached the Great Plains, but states west of the Rockies were eighty percent free. Mexico was overrun, but Canada was hanging on thanks mainly to the fall frost. Lucky bastards. But the cold would our saving grace—we just didn't know it yet.

A large mob of zombies approached Philly. So-called experts claimed that they were mostly former NYC residents. It had only been eight months, and they'd traveled a hundred miles. Then came the stories of forts like ours that had it worse. The New Orleans Superdome was renamed the "Dome of Death" because it only held out for three weeks before people holed up there started killing each other, and within hours thousands had joined the undead. The newly appointed president used this story to show we must work together if we wanted to survive this mess. How were we gonna survive when the mob arrived here? We were barely 800 strong. What about the navy? Most of the ships had run out of food long ago and had turned to piracy out of desperation. How was that working together? Sure they tried to slow the mob by shelling them when they had the chance, but the subs wouldn't in good conscience add to the US's radioactive waste. And most were not responding. America's once-proud arsenal of nuclear warheads were corroding in their silos because the warriors who'd manned them were gone. So the crazy idea of nuking ourselves was out the window. Meanwhile, the new president continued rambling on about the status of our great country and how we would overcome this catastrophe. He concluded that you could head west during the winter and get to Denver, the new capital. A warm body in Denver is better than a cold one on the streets. How lame was that? Over the coming weeks passed, we'd occasionally have an attack on the two east gates, but none as bad that night.

CHAPTER 1

First Winter

Winter came fast and struck with a vengeance, dropping to twenty-six below in the middle of November. Everyone was getting sick. Medicine was running low, and while we had plenty of food, the flu shots were gone, and we had ten percent of the antibiotics of what we should have had on hand. So many people were sick in bed that we were standing eighteen hours on and eighteen hours off, due the shortage of both men and beds. That first week of December we lost about thirty people, mainly the elderly, to the flu. It was a hard month, and it was going to get harder. The fires to the north were finally out, and the sun was beginning to break through the clouds. The cold was getting colder, the thermometers stopped at forty below, and there were several nights colder than that.

That's when the policy of sharing homes to conserve warmth went into effect. Housing was cramped enough, but now it was ridiculous—I think twenty people to a four-bedroom house at one point. Thank God for the Humvees. They could get through the snow, but guards on foot and zombies could barely move. We had to plow a path around the fence for the sentries who walked in pairs.

It was around this time that our sole primary function began to end as we began to run out of raw material and had to start melting scrap iron. Artillery Park was disassembled to add to the scrap iron to replenish shells, but where to get gunpowder? We still communicated with headquarters, but they were more concerned with themselves. Go figure. That's when we realized we were on our own. There was a reservist armory about ten miles to the south in Coal Valley, and another sixty miles to the north in Galena. But we had no way of getting there, nor did we even know if they had ammo.

The cold had knocked us off our perfect island. The river froze, making almost the entire east side vulnerable, but luckily the ice wasn't thick enough for zombies to cross. A few still tried, and we let them test the waters. None were successful. As winter ended in late March, we knew we'd be out of fuel by summer. Food was still plentiful, and while medicine was dangerously low, it would last longer than fuel.

We held two town meetings—one military and one civilian. At the civilian meeting, they demanded to know what was going to be done about the rotting corpses from our dead and the dead outside the gates. A prominent "doctor" stated that if something wasn't done, we'd get sicker. We respected the second generation Indian dentist; he was my dentist when I was a small child. The military meeting was more serious. We all knew the fuel situation. The idea of using horses was dismissed because where would we get them? We needed fuel and medicine.

That's when my buddy, Chuck, came up with the idea of a suicide squad. Everyone was shocked. Was he serious? Supposedly a bunch of guys could cross the bridge and get what we needed. I mean, we talked about it, but to actually do it would be crazy. Col. Majors said he would consider it if it was our only option.

It was agreed that an air drop would have limited success because the island presented a small target surrounded by water—if headquarters would even help out. We'd heard stories about "headquarters" dropping supplies from a forward air base in the Dakotas. We Midwesterners must be stubborn people because we didn't want their help any longer. So on the bulletin board the next day was a volunteer list. My name was third on the list. Out of the remaining 250 or so military remaining, twenty-two of us volunteered. I was the second-most senior member to volunteer, so I was tasked with establishing guidelines and rules. One guy chickened out, so the remaining twenty-one of us were pulled off of standing shifts. We started training and became very proficient with weapons other than guns.

During this time, we started planting crops anywhere they might grow—the golf course, Artillery Park, and even the graveyard. It was mainly so the civilians could give back. We burned the bodies of the dead and the smell was horrible. Even now I still smell the burning flesh.

As the snow melted, attacks on the east gates began to pick up. Col. Majors finally started showing signs that the job was getting to him, and we began to see more of Capt. Lewis as he gradually assumed the colonel's daily duties. He decided to start drills to prepare us for the inevitable zombie break-through, mostly at night around 3 a. m. Sirens originally meant for air raids would sound, and all military personnel would assemble in the motor pool. Civilians would assemble in the theater, hospital, and gym, all stone buildings that had been reinforced with steel. They were stocked with enough food for a week.

The suicide squad would monitor from headquarters. The off-watch section would go to the primary scene, while the section that would normally be sleeping would be split in two, with half going to protect the civilians, and the other half going to the far-side sections to allow those men to better arm themselves. Once they were armed, they would relieve the more poorly armed sectors. The drills sucked badly, but after awhile they became standard practice and we were used to them.

Finally June First arrived—the day we were to "roll out." The plan was simple: the helicopters would circle over head and find three tanker trucks and two tractor trailers. Meanwhile, three Hummers with sixteen guys in them would proceed from the west bridge into Davenport, Iowa, and the bridge would quickly open back up. The two helicopters had the remaining four guys in them. They found a tanker about three blocks west of the bridge. Sgt. Johnston and Sgt. Harris roped down from the bird, and jackpot! The keys were in it, and the tanker was about three-quarters full. Johnston started it on the third try. Harris was sitting on the top of the cab when he spotted two figures in the distance. He shouted to them, and there was no response. He fired two clean shots, and they went down.

Meanwhile, the Hummers raced to the tanker, and after stalling out twice, they got it to the bridge. Lt. Lewis(no relation to Capt. Lewis)made it policy that we were to check for stowaways under the vehicle, so they were stopped on the center part of the bridge while it was swung out and inspected. When they were finished, they made it to the safe side and parked.

Johnston and Harris, meanwhile, got back into their bird. The other bird had found a tanker about ten blocks northwest of the bridge. Cpl. Wallace and Sgt. Brown roped down to it. Wallace made the mistake of opening the door without checking inside, and a zombie leaped out and bit him in the neck. Wallace fell back, spewing blood all over the street. Brown, on top of the cab, stared in shock as his partner lay dying. The chopper pilot, Hawkeye, called down to Brown, who hesitated as the zombie trucker hopped out of the cab and started chewing on Wallace's leg.

Brown opened fire, unloading a fifteen-round magazine at his friend and the zombie. Brown reloaded and thought about making sure there were no other zombies. He swept the area and saw none. He checked the cab and found the keys in the ignition. He tried to start it, but the fuel tank was dry. It appears the zombie trucker had left the engine running. Brown radioed Lt. Lewis asking what to do. Lt. Lewis said, "Get up top and see how much fuel is in the tanker." A few minutes later, Brown radioed that it was completely full.

When Lewis and the Hummers arrived, Chuck siphoned gas from the tanker. We knew we didn't have much time because the tractor was a diesel and the fuel in the tanker was regular unleaded. We hauled ass to the bridge. The three Hummers went to the safe side while the truck parked on the center section. Chuck and Brown swept the truck clean, the whole process taking three hours.

We had about seven hours of safe daylight, so Chuck joined Brown in the second helicopter. The two choppers went out twenty blocks without finding any good prospects. We decided risk trying to find an empty tanker and found one about fifteen blocks south by the riverboats. We'd checked it out a few hours earlier and found the cab to be in good condition but the tanker empty. The birds went back to the base to get a sump pump. The plan was to pump diesel from the nearest gas station into the tank.

We had two hours. On the way to the tanker, I heard over the CB radio, "Where are all the zombies?" We were about to find out that the nearby riverboats were a zombie haven. While we were pumping gas at a station on the corner by the Isle of Capri, we surrounded the fuel truck with the Hummers.

The sun had started to set, and both choppers were circling overhead. That's when Hawkeye noticed movement on the riverboats. He shined his spotlight down and saw that they were covered with them—close to 400, the pilot reported, telling us to haul ass. The tanker truck was roughly two-thirds full and Lt. Lewis got greedy. We had enough fuel for a few months, but he was the ranking officer, so we stayed. The sun was almost gone. "We have to go!" I screamed to Lt. Lewis.

"Contact six o'clock," chirped the radio. The .50 cal opened up on something moving. Whatever it was, it was gone. After Chuck and Brown put the sump pump in the helo, they jumped into the cab and hit the lights. They lit the darkness and probably ten zombies about three blocks down, then took off toward the bridge. The three Hummers loaded up, and the second bird radioed down to get a move on. The zombies on the top of the riverboat were falling into the water or onto the land below and were moving toward us. Lt. Lewis's Hummer was the last in the convoy.

What I know is, that Hummer was still sitting there when I left. The pilot told them to move, but what he saw was three zombies coming out of the darkness, punching through the passenger window, and pulling the lieutenant out of the Hummer. The noises I heard next will be forever burned into

my mind—of Lt. Lewis being torn limb from limb, screaming for his life. The Hummer raced off. The .50 cal let loose
a series of shots, presumably to end his misery.

After we all arrived at the bridge, each vehicle was inspected, starting with the truck and Lt. Lewis's former Hummer. They were clean. Our Hummers were parked facing
opposite directions. The second helicopter was following
the zombie gamblers, and the pack was moving toward us—
about 200 of them, he guessed. The gunner in the bird tried
to slow them down, but his gun jammed. They weren't going
to be any help to us now.

The bridge was still swinging when Capt. Lewis ordered
it stopped. He said we brought this on ourselves, convenient
after we'd just brought him so much gas.

We positioned the Hummers in a line to form a defensive barrier—the ten of us versus close to 200 zombies. Each
man said a prayer. One helo continued to track the zombie
pack while the other quickly refueled and returned to open
fire on them, shining his light up and down the block behind
us as he fired. We needed to make our shots count, so we
waited until we could smell the stink of death. The .50 cals
fired first, and the first row was shredded. Then we started
firing, taking turns reloading. The only way to get back to the
Rock was through the dead army.

The helo was contributing so much that we would have
died without him. It seemed like the more we killed, the
more appeared in windows and joined their undead brothers. After fifteen minutes, the Hummer I was riding in ran
out of ammo. About a minute later, the other one did too.
I shoved my last magazine into the M16 and knew I had to
make the thirty shots count. I wasn't the only one almost
without ammo.

I made the decision to pull back. We each had about three-
quarters of a tank of gas, so we all piled into our Hummers
and took off away from the pack. Our plan was to lead them
away and double back. It seemed like the plan might work.
The one helo shined down on us like an angel from above.

The second stayed with the pack, but he too was running out of ammo. We drove about seven blocks and stopped, shining lights everywhere. Nothing. It was too calm.

The second copter had used all its ammo. He continued telling us the zombies were still in hot pursuit of the trucks and were trying to cross the open bridge. By now, Chuck had rearmed, as had an entire shift of guards. They were begging Capt. Lewis to save us because we were sitting ducks in the middle of the road. I ordered the helo to come down and load up the guys. Those in the first Humvee gave their ammo to Sgt. Avery, Cpl. Simpson, Cpl. Black, and me, then jumped into the bird. We'd hold out till it came back. The pilot said he'd be back in twenty minutes. We knew it would be longer. I took the wheel because I grew up on the other side of the water and was slightly familiar with the roads.

Chuck had woken up Col. Majors, who was almost on his death bed. He agreed with Capt. Lewis's decision, to not open the bridge any further. Chuck was beyond pissed. He didn't want to leave us out there to die. He got to thinking the bridge was twenty-five degrees off from forming a perfect line. He got a rope and slung it across. There was no way it would stay. The winch from the Humvee wasn't going to work. "Contact, Sector One," the radio chirped—as if my night couldn't get worse. The shift commander said, ever so calmly, "Report threat."

"Minor," replied Sector One. The squad leaders broke from Chuck, as did several of the guards.

I radioed to the helo over the bridge to report Sector Three. He flew over the island. "Non-existent," he said. That was an open window, but I would have to drive back toward the riverboat across the I-74 bridge, then through downtown Moline or Rock Island.

Four months earlier, we'd watched the Centennial Bridge collapse when a tugboat drifted into the support beam and left us with only using the I-74 bridge. The problem was, I-74 was full of cars, some with zombies who couldn't get out of them. The final nail in our coffin came as we sat on the corner of West and 72nd street. A burned-out 7-Elevenwas on the corner, where a pack of dogs were busy eating something living.

Capt. Lewis's voice came over the CB, "Hawkeye Two, report to base. All flights are grounded."

"Are you trying to kill us?" I yelled into the mic. There was no reply.

"I'm sorry, Logan," said Chuck. "There's nothing we can do. They're at all three sectors. We need the air support. I hope you understand." I understood, so I copied. He said, "Stay alive, and we'll get you in the a. m."—eight hours away at the soonest, since it was only 10:30 p. m. Fucking Chuck. He'd suggested this, and tonight he was gonna sleep safe in his bed on the Rock. Nobody said anything—we just sat there.

Black saw it first. The building was half collapsed, but what was left looked solid. The windows were barred. Above the door were two crossed swords. It was a long shot, but it was our best bet. We backed the Hummer to the door and left Simpson in it with the engine running. He had every light shining toward the street for the first sign of trouble. We flicked on our flashlights as we entered. Inside we found our first break of the night. Nearly untouched was every type of ammo we needed—no .50 cal ammo, though. The building was surprisingly clear. Each of the men were exhausted and extremely cautious so, it took three hours to load the trunk, and we took turns watching for signs of zombies. The downside was, we had all this ammo and no magazines. I think we had six empty ones. But there was still plenty of ammo left in the store." We'll come back here," I told them.

"If they let us," Avery said.

"Oh they will," I said.

We set out for the other Hummer, and as we rounded the first corner, we smashed into three zombies. Two folded in half like lawn chairs, and the third smashed into the passenger window. Simpson yelled to run him over. Black gunned the engine, and we heard bones crunching.

It was hard to see the other Hummer at first because it was surrounded by maybe fifty zombies. Black rammed it into reverse and stepped on the gas to get away from them. We drove around and went back to the bridge. There were fifteen zombies standing there. We radioed in that we needed the bridge, then quickly dispatched the undead. Luckily the guard in the bridge shack was sympathetic and aligned the bridge so we could cross over to the island.

Before we even made it to the other side, Capt. Lewis was standing there, yelling at us for our stupidity. The next morning, the entire suicide squad was ordered to Col. Majors office. Even though his health was failing, he was still able to convey how pissed he was about the whole ordeal—but he was grateful for the results. It was decided that Lt. Greene was our new leader, and we'd have to work on our tactics. That day we began an official boot camp, to hopefully to prevent ever suffering losses again.

CHAPTER 2

Fall

We'd fought off a few zombie attacks, nothing serious. But we'd perfected our tactics for raiding Davenport. We scavenged all the supplies during this time frame without any losses. We cleaned out a lot of zombies and wild animals. By then, dogs had become aggressive toward us. They avoided the zombies, even though the zombies never tried to eat them.

Supplies in Davenport and Bettendorf, Iowa, were almost gone, thanks largely to the fire that had started during a freak summer lightning strike. We didn't have enough food, medicine, or gas to get through the winter, so we put together a final push to get the supplies we'd need. The plan had three phases. The first was to train about twenty additional people as a contingent of drivers and guards for seven big rigs. Four semis had been were "tricked out"—mounted with two .50 cals on the top of the trailer. The doors of each cab were reinforced, and the side windows were covered with a layer of sheet metal. The front of the cabs had barbed wire across the grill and hood. The tankers were not armed, but we had eight Hummers to protect the convoy. That was the second phase in our grand plan.

We brought along a bobcat to load the trailers faster and planned to bring several dozen pallets to stack boxes on. Any ammo that couldn't be used for our weapons was used to make new bullets in the now defunct ammo factory. Phase three was going to be more difficult than "tricking out" a few semis and teaching basic combat. We used three bulldozers to clear a path from the Rock to the I-74 bridge and off onto the Avenue of the Cities. There were about 200 cars along the four-mile stretch, almost all of them on the bridge. Evidently on the trek west, the plague had been carried along every major highway, and the great Eisenhower Interstate System had become an accelerant for the "army of death." It took about four days of careful work to clear the bridge and the on-off ramps. Several dozen cars still had families of zombies in them. Once the route was cleared, we set a date at the end of October, to make sure everything was squared away.

The night before, we had a massive feast for the 692 people on the Rock, and Lt. Greene led a kind of church service. It had been at least four months since we'd heard from headquarters. We knew there was some sort of military presence out there because we'd heard planes fly overhead.

The last word from President Bishop, the elected president before the world went to shit, was that the US government had relocated Denver and that Los Angeles had been isolated. While there had been minor outbreaks, but thanks to unity the West was oddly safe, considering how many people called So Cal home. He urged all citizens to stay strong and promised that help was coming. He talked about the strength of Cleveland, where close to 2,000 survivors were staying strong until what passed for the air force was able to evacuate all of them. The zombie pack had grown in size, and as a result of flyovers, their numbers were estimated to range from 500,000 to two million. They were approaching Cleveland, and that's why he'd ordered the evacuation. He was convinced that the 2,000 would not last against an army of that size.

He'd talked about the major outposts still left—St. Paul, Chicago, Gary, Nashville, Cincy, Detroit, Baton Rouge, Little Rock, and Atlanta—"government-sanctioned" forts. The rest were considered holdouts, and the government couldn't afford to spend the limited resources on everybody. He said he wanted to help everyone, but due to the limited resources the needs of the majority outweighed the wants of the few survivors. He'd concluded by saying that a liberation plan was in the works, and by mid-spring it would be in effect. "Just hold out," he'd urged us all.

After that speech, everyone was unified that we had to continue with the raids. We wouldn't last the summer, but that was four months ago, and winter was approaching. That night, no one could sleep because the tension in the air was so thick you could cut it with a knife. Then, at 4 a. m., the sirens sounded. It wasn't an attack, it was a drill to prepare the base for that dreadful day. Fifty-one of us assembled in the security area. By now we no longer wore uniforms; it was an eclectic mix of fatigues and hunting outfits.

Tensions were still high as I mounted the lead Hummer, with Lt. Greene in the rear Hummer. I was in the passenger seat, and behind me was the mission navigator, our communications expert. We radio-checked several dozen times before we got through the gate. The convoy was ordered this way: two Hummers, followed by a tanker, two semis, two more Hummers, a tanker, two semis, two Hummers, a tanker and the last two Hummers. The plan was to conserve as much ammo as possible, so unless there were several targets, nobody was to fire. Unlike the early days, everyone now understood the importance of our situation.

Once off the swing bridge, we headed north toward I-74. We got on the on-ramp and then onto the bridge. Not a zombie in sight. The two helos were flying overhead and reported smooth sailing until the Avenue of the Cities. The Avenue was chosen because of its close proximity to I-74. There were four gas stations right off the interstate, where precious diesel fuel was sold. Each tanker was going to go to a different station, where it would connect its sump pump and start pumping. Five of the Hummers would break off and protect the essentially defenseless tankers. There were three supermarkets on the Avenue, about a mile from the off-ramp. The remaining Hummers and all four semis headed for one while the tankers were sent back to the Rock without waiting for the semis. The Hummers would follow to the Rock and double back.

Loading the semis was a slow, boring process. We went to the first grocery store, and all four backed up to the front doors. Then I went inside with the Hummer crew, and we cleared the store. A few of us stood guard while the rest loaded food, medicine, and other various supplies onto the pallets.

About an hour into it, the first zombie appeared. It was quickly dispatched by a single shot to the head. Then ten minutes later we heard from one of the tankers that it had suffered a blowout on its way back to the Rock and slid off the interstate. A plan was devised that would send the other tankers all but two Hummers back to base while two Hummers stayed with the disabled tanker. The Hummers would return with two bulldozers to pull the tanker back onto the pavement.

We started to fall behind our schedule, so I ordered two of the guards to help load food because we had to move on. After we finished, we went to the next store, about a half a block away. As before, we backed up the trucks and cleared the building. The guys on the back machine guns were told to get out and help with the loading. Maybe it was the fact that we were less nervous, but the mood was quite jovial. That lasted all of two minutes, until Chuck broke radio silence. He was in charge of the tanker rescue. He called out, "We got a large mob coming from the east. They're on all sides. Advise." Greene ran over to me and we conferred. I ordered the helos to fly over and provide air cover.

"How long until the other three Hummers and bulldozers get there?" I asked Chuck. He had no idea. Nobody was answering, so fearing the worst, we told them to load up in their Hummers and come to us.

"Lieutenant, we got a bit of a problem," Hawkeye radioed with some hesitation.

"What kind of problem?"

"There's more than a few zombies. Try a few thousand." Everyone's heart dropped. Was this the beginning of the mob? We wouldn't last long without food. The trucks were a little over two-thirds full. That would probably get us through winter, but fuel would be limited.

"ETA?" Greene asked.

"At this rate, they should reach the tanker in about an hour," the pilot replied calmly. "But that's the main body of the pack. There are some stragglers out front." Greene and I agreed that we would continue working for about thirty more minutes, then take off. The lieutenant informed the base of our situation, and the Rock replied that the tankers were almost to the base. But there was no way the bulldozers would reach the crippled tanker. Chuck's .50 cal could be heard in the distance. He called and said just a few speed bumps. About fifteen minutes later, the last of the pallets were staged. Everyone mounted up. As we rolled onto the streets, Chuck's Humvee raced up and blocked us and he opened his door. The tanker's former driver got out and jumped inside a semi.

"I'm tired of riding, Bitch. Can we go now?" Chuck said with chuckle. I smiled. He could still joke, knowing what lay ahead.

The helos were returning with more ammo after refueling. "How far?" Greene asked the birds.

"They should reach the off-ramp in about twenty minutes," one pilot replied. We raced toward the interstate. The helos were instructed to keep the mob from blocking the off-ramp. In five minutes, we were on the highway. The three Hummers coming from the Rock called to report that they were approaching the I-74 bridge. We instructed them to take a defensive position. The helos opened fire, but they were right over us.

From the lead Hummer I saw thirty or so coming down the embankment up ahead. More and more started spilling down onto the highway. It felt like the zombies had set up an ambush, but that was impossible, so it had to be pure coincidence. We kept pressing ahead. The highway was gradually getting clogged with dead. We accelerated to get through them, but there were getting to be too many bodies on the road. Still, we kept pushing. This was by far the worst encounter we'd had. The rear Hummer called and said it was starting to affect their ability to negotiate the road.

Then the roadway started to rise about a quarter mile ahead. *Safety! We can make it*, I thought. The helos were rattling away. Every gun was firing at the mob. Finally we broke through their lines, but the entire convoy was still jammed up. I ordered the semis to keep going. It would be smooth sailing for them. My Hummer stopped, and we used the .50 cal to thin what we could. The other Hummers did the same thing, but the driver of the next to last Hummer had Chuck in it. Then, Chuck radioed that the last three Hummers were stuck and couldn't make it because the bodies were too deep. The swarm moved around the three stranded Hummers, as if they could sense the danger their food was in, because they stopped advancing on us and turned around and headed for the stranded vehicles.

"They're climbing on the back of them!" yelled one of the pilots. Steve Oliver, a hell of a mechanic, was the first one they grabbed. They ripped him limb from limb. The other two .50 cal gunners climbed into the vehicles and sealed the hatches.

"Go. No sense in you watching this," Chuck said somberly. I didn't want to believe it, but there was no way to stem the tide. We fired and fired, but there were too many of them.

"We gotta go," the lieutenant said. I couldn't leave him, Chuck waited for me. We heard smashing glass. It was the end.

"*Go!*" Chuck said.

"I can't"—my words breaking up as I said them.

"Things happen. But you have to go. I've got a plan." We took off. The driver of one of the other Hummers was screaming for us to come back, but we knew they were done for the minute they stopped moving. As I watched the swarm, the helos tried desperately to fend off the undead. Just as we reached the bridge, we heard an explosion. We stopped. Somehow Chuck's Hummer had exploded, taking out one of the other Hummers and probably hundreds of zombies with it.

"Fucking Chuck," the lieutenant said. Chuck had always been a pyro. *Fitting end to our firebug*, I thought. The rest of the ride was somber. We came back with about eighty percent of the food we wanted, and two-thirds the fuel we needed—at a cost of thirteen men. Nine of the thirteen were part of the original squad, and only half of the original members remained. More importantly, one of my good friends was gone.

As we got to the Rock, people greeted us and started to unload the food. I went to my bed and laid down. I woke three hours later to the sound of the air raid siren. A drill? *Now*? Assholes. Then I heard Capt. Lewis over the PA. "This is not a drill. We have a breakthrough, Zone A," his amplified voice echoed. Crap. We were all so drained.

Most of the Hummers we'd used today, along with the ammo, were in the security of the motor pool. I ran to my spot. Drills were supposed to prepare us for everything, but this all seemed new to everyone. The shift commander was freaking out, but Luckily, Lt. Greene showed up and calmly told him to let him run the show.

The breakthrough wasn't bad—it's just that there were so many they'd overwhelmed the fence. We began to push them back as bodies started piling up. After a few hours, we finally stemmed the tide, and the zombies were locked out for now. The next morning, Capt. Lewis called an emergency meeting to review the island's defenses. Without much argument, we agreed that it would be in our best interest to block off or, better yet, destroy the two bridges from Moline.

The plan we worked out was simple: blow up the bridge supports, using what little C-4 we had left. Someone would row up to the support base in a boat, plant the C-4, and boom. We all gathered along the fence to watch as two guys I barely knew, supposedly experts in blowing things up, were given the job. As they approached the first bridge, zombies sensed them and started jumping. The first dozen were way off, then a few would get close to the boat as it got closer to the bridge. We told them to come back and get a motor boat, maybe a waste of precious fuel. As the boat started to turn around, a zombie child, probably eight years old, landed on the boat.

We heard the sound of crunching bones as the child's legs, arms, and other brittle bones broke. We hadn't thought of that happening. They started bashing her head in with the oars as the current pulled them closer to the bridge. Unaware of the inevitable, they were surprised when two zombies landed onto the boat and started to rip them apart. The boat drifted into the base of the bridge, then lazily broke free and rammed the opposite shore. The zombies on the boat started rocking it enough to capsize it and spill our valuable C-4 into the murky waters.

Now we needed a new plan. We had some old grenades and the helo had about six rockets. This time we used a motor boat, and the zombies immediately started jumping again. But this boat moved too fast. We duct-taped about half the grenades to each bridge support. Then the helo took aim and leveled both bridges.

We were now out of grenades and rockets, but at least we were safe on the island again—or so we thought. That night two separate patrols were attacked by six half-charred zombies. One guy was bitten, but the zombies were quickly destroyed. The problem was, the guy who was bitten didn't tell anyone. We found out this sad fact about two days later when he didn't show up for his shift. He stayed in that night with what he said was the flu. But sometime during the night he had turned and started devouring his wife. He moved onto his three little girls, and then the other family that shared the house with him. Luckily he and his undead companions were contained inside the house and their bodies were quickly incinerated. The rest of his patrol was stripped to make sure no one else was bitten. One man had killed nine people on the island because of his selfishness. Rules were made about reporting people with flu-like symptoms.

Winter came and life was good now that both bridges had been blown. The east side was well protected because the river ice wasn't as strong as last year. Food was in good enough supply and might last until midsummer. Gas was used sparingly. As winter drew to a close, there were about 600 of us on the base. We were able to tune into the president. Almost all bases east of the Mississippi had been overrun or evacuated. There were still a few strongholds in Chicago and Nashville. The army was preparing to clear out the zombies by the end of the year—already six months later than originally promised. So Cal was declared cleared, and most of the West would be by summer. The president said broadcasts were short because there weren't many people left to reach. We'd tried contacting other survivors in several ways, without success. No planes flew overhead either, so we were alone against the undead. The pack seemed to have been thinned out by aerial attacks from the few remaining air force bombers, destroying a few thousand zombies. Those remaining moved slowly toward us. Not much of the news was any use to us.

CHAPTER 3

Spring

It was time to start planning for the summer. The first thing we had to do was prepare everyone for what was to come. The zombies were getting hungrier and hungrier. They were lining the east shore and the bridge entrance into Davenport. To make matters worse, one of the two helicopters couldn't sustain altitude. Without any parts, or real mechanics to service them, it was useless. Two years of flying on the wrong fuel had taken its toll.

If we did nothing, we'd be out of gas by July and food by December. The golf course had been turned into a farm for corn and other produce—not enough to sustain us, but it was something. The use of Hummers was limited to the island when absolutely necessary, so we had to walk everywhere— or, if we got lucky, use an electric golf cart.

We tore down some old cinderblock buildings block by block to build an eight-to-ten-foot tall wall along the east side. Col. Majors had finally become a figurehead—nobody ever saw him besides Capt. Lewis. We'd completed one fuel run and brought back two tankers without a hitch. The simplest way to get to the other side was to load up on the two-and-a-half-ton truck, we found in the island museum and drive backwards through the crowd to the bridge and clear a path. Once the convoy passed through, the deuce-and-a-half went back to base.

We began to prepare for another fuel run about a week later. It was just after six p. m., and I'd just finished eating when the sirens sounded.

"Breach in Sector Seven," said the shift commander. I really wasn't in the mood for a drill. "Breach in Sector Six. This is not a drill." I ran to the security office and started arming up.

"What's going on?" I asked. Somehow the zombies had overwhelmed the chain-link fence. It wasn't a lot of them, but enough to push over the fence. After the first siren, more frantic radio comms were coming about the zombies and how they were approaching. The shots became more sporadic as we arrived on the scene—the zombies had overtaken the patrols and were inching their way inland. We started firing into the mob, and they started to thin out.

"Where did they all come from?" someone shouted from behind. After about two hours, the patrols continued and we helped clean up the corpses. That's when Brandon Williams, a member of the original guards, noticed that one of zombies looked like someone we knew as Mike. Made sense because Mike was in one of the three Hummers that the zombies got a hold of. We burned the bodies, and the stink of burning dead flesh was horrible.

That exercise woke everyone up, and we finished the concrete wall in a matter of days. It was exhausting work, but it had to be done. We'd be safer because the zombies had gotten smarter or luckier and had started walking underwater. It was still spring, and that meant we had to go on raids sans helicopters. The helicopters were falling apart due to neglect. The zombies were crowded around the bridge entrance. We now faced the basic problem of getting across the bridge through what seemed like a thousand zombies, which prevented the deuce-and-a-half from doing its job.

We were in the conference room discussing ways to get it done when someone in the back said, "Like the Marines did in World War Two." It was Ryan Rumler, a former jarhead. We were curious, so he explained that it would involve salvaging two barges and a tug from upriver.

Three barges and a tugboat were easily savaged, the third barge set up as a spare. The barges were rigged with ramps to get the vehicles on and off. We spent two weeks working on a plan that probably wouldn't work. We trained and prepared for a landing outside the old boat ramp by the old Case plant. We still monitored the shortwave radio in hopes of finding out what was happening in the world. As expected, nothing. Big surprise.

The night before we set out, we ate like kings—well, as much as canned goods allowed. We went over our plan. We had four semis and two tankers again, but only three Hummers—not because we lacked vehicles, but because we were down to about 575 people and couldn't spare very many people for this mission. The semis would head south toward the Super Wal-Mart, and the tankers would go to the three gas stations next to the old Case plant. We loaded up in the wee hours, and at first light we unloaded.

The semis and two Hummers raced toward Wal-Mart, while the remaining Hummer went to the gas stations a block away. After six tense hours, the last semi departed Wal-Mart and was on the barge within twenty-five minutes. Success— we got enough fuel and food to last through most of fall. One more run like this and we'd be set till spring. We decided two runs would be better.

The next run would be in ten days. Until then we reorganized the defense of the island. Of the 575 people, only 275 were able to fight. Close to 200 were kids fourteen and under. The rest were either still shell-shocked or too old to help. We referred to them as shell-shocked because even after two years they were still unable to accept the reality of our situation. We locked them in the old reserve center, which cost us six people from island defense, but it was better to lock them up because a few of them had tried to swim across the river. Needless to say, they quickly realized their mistake.

We decided to make a third trip for building supplies. We'd also extend the wall farther around the island. This would reduce the number of people required to guard the island and allow for more down time. The plan was simple—we'd do one food and fuel run in ten days, and fifteen days later we'd do a run for cinder blocks, cement, etc. Then fifteen days after that we'd top off the food and fuel. But the fuel from the very last run would have to stay in the tankers, because the tanks on the island tanks would be full.

Ten days later, as before, we landed at the boat ramp and raided the local area. The only trouble we had was when one semi had to smash through a random cluster of zombies surrounding a corner house. They heard a gunshot almost simultaneously, and one of the tires blew. Luckily the driver maintained control, and the truck plowed into a few zombies and continued on its way. When the driver and the rest of the convoy arrived, he told us about his encounter. We discussed it for a few minutes and decided to take a look at the house. When we found it, it was apparent that something was inside. All the lower windows were boarded up and about fifty zombies were clawing at the house. Before we could get any closer, a shot rang out and hit the other Hummer's window. We stopped and used the PA.

"We come in peace. Show yourself. We can help." Silence. We waited for about ten minutes. That's about how long it took the zombies to notice us. We knew they'd follow us back to the boat ramp, so we killed a handful. "We're leaving," I said via the PA. "We'll pass by in about three weeks. If you want sanctuary, give us a sign." We went back to the river, got onto the barge and cast off. As we pulled into the Rock, we tied up and got the tankers off first so they could head to the fuel depot. Then the food-laden semis pulled off and headed to the staging area, where they'd be unloaded the next day.

The sun was already setting. As the driver of one of the semis stepped down, he felt the sharp pain in his leg and looked down to see a zombie head firmly attached to it. He screamed out in pain and pulled out a bowie knife and plunged it into the creature's head. Then he ran over to Lt. Jon Greene and pleaded with him to let him see his little girl one more time. Greene and two other men loaded him into a Hummer, and that was the last we saw of him. I hope he got to see his little girl. I never did ask Jon about it. Looking back, I should have.

We finished unloading the supplies around 2 a. m. The next few days went by quietly and quickly. We started preps for the run for building supplies. We decided the best two locations were the Lowe's next to Wal-Mart and the Home Depot in Iowa. That would be the deepest we ever went into Iowa. A few miles up from the base was a landing dock that would be perfect. We were working out the details, when I heard someone say, "What about that house in Illinois?"

"We did make a promise to them, so we should check on them," Jon said. We decided to take the last working helicopter out in two days. We prayed it would fly. When we finally wrapped up, I went to get some sleep.

In the morning, two would-be mechanics, Bill and Jesse, and I looked at the helo to see if it would work. It started okay and took off and landed fine. The next day, Jon, Hawkeye, another pilot and me took off for that house and to do some recon. We flew over the Home Depot and Lowe's, and both appeared to be intact. We then proceeded to our landing area for the next run. It too was all clear, so we started toward the house. We were midway over the river when an alarm sounded from the helo's instrument panel.

"We've lost hydraulics," the co-pilot said, looking back at us. We were going down.

"I've lost rudder control," Hawkeye yelled. A split second later, the cold, rushing water hit me like a dream. The next fifteen seconds felt like an eternity as I tried to unbuckle my seat belt. I looked down and saw a light flashing—Jon cutting my harness. There was blood drifting from cockpit area. At first it was a surreal scene, as if the pilots were fighting against some unseen monster. Then Jon grabbed me and pulled me to the surface and we swam toward the Illinois side of the river. Once we were on land, we sat on a park bench with our backs to each other. We waited for the pilots to break the surface of the water and they never came.

About thirty minutes passed before Jon broke the silence. "How do you think we're going to get back?"

"I don't know," I said, shivering. I stood up and started walking toward a swing set. On the ground there was a GI

Joe action figure. I picked it up and inspected it. I put it in my cargo pocket. If we made it home, I could give it to some kid.

Jon stood up and walked toward the river. He picked up a few rocks and threw them into the water. "We gotta get moving," he said. We started toward the road and found an abandoned Jeep Grand Cherokee. After three years, it still started, and we started down the road toward the on-ramp. As we got to the ramp, we encountered a handful of zombies. Since we only had a 9mm pistol, we figured we'd avoid them. It was weird though—they were surrounding a car. Was there someone in it? We inched closer and got about fifteen feet away, and Jon and I took aim at two zombies. The other five realized that something was different and proceeded toward us. We dropped them with ease. We got out of the Jeep and started walking toward the car, and as we got about three feet away, the passenger door flew open and a teenage girl jumped out and came running toward us, crying. She hugged Jon and said thank you about a hundred times.

We put her in the back of the Jeep and continued onto the I-74 bridge, making it to Iowa without a hitch. We tried to get the guards attention and finally, after ten minutes the bridge started to groan. Jon lined up the Jeep with the bridge and floored it, and we rammed into a small huddle of zombies by the bridge. When we broke through, Jon gunned it toward the slowly shutting bridge. He slammed on the brakes and we all jumped out. There were still zombies around us, but we quickly dodged them. The zombies now started toward us, and seeing this, the guards started to reopen the bridge.

We were all exhausted from the cold, but I drew on my last bit of strength and ran faster. The girl fell back. Jon and I were almost to the gap as bullets started bouncing around us. The guards were firing at *us*, and we were yelling at them to stop. We heard a scream and turned around to see the girl go down. I started to head back, but Jon grabbed me. About six zombies had already reached her and were feasting on her juicy flesh. We jumped onto the open bridge span and then crawled onto the stationary part of the bridge to the safety of the island. The girl's screams were still audible as the guards easily picked off the six zombies that were enjoying their last meal.

Jon walked up to the bridge operator. "What the fuck is your problem?" he demanded.

Just then, Capt. Lewis came from behind the wall. "I wanted them to take you cowboys out. Maybe now you'll be more careful. I'd figure after the incident where we lost thirty men and several piles of equipment, you'd learn. But obviously I was wrong. So, effective immediately, nobody is allowed to leave the base."

"What about supplies?" Jon asked.

"We have plenty," Lewis quipped.

"Bullshit. They're getting onto the island because we don't have a wall, and they know this," Jon said.

"So you're telling me that these brain-dead suckers have figured out how to get onto the island?" Lewis said.

"They've been doing that for years," I said.

"So, what good is a wall gonna do now?" Lewis asked.

"What *good*?" Jon demanded.

"Because every time one of you mavericks decides to jump the fence, you put me and my island at risk," remarked Lewis.

"*Your* island?" yelled Jon.

"Yes. The United States of America put me in command to defend its interest," he said dryly.

"I don't know if you noticed, but the U-S-of-A doesn't give a flying fuck about us," Jon said as he started walking away.

"They do. While you were out swimming, I received a shortwave call from Force General Scudheigh. We're to evacuate and proceed to Bismarck, North Dakota, to be integrated into the Force Army Corps," he said. That sent shivers up my spine. Scudheigh was a vile man. He'd tricked several hundred people to leave their homes, and when they arrived where he'd sent them, he'd ambush, rape, kill, and eat them. We eventually found out who he was, thanks to a message from President Bishop—about two months too late.

"When were you gonna share this?" I asked.

"And it's a horrible idea," Jon said, coming back over.

"Orders are orders. We're supposed to meet up with the reserves from Galena and Cedar Rapids in a place called Marshalltown, where the 7th Air Rescue Squadron will evacuate us." Lewis then went off to address the Rock, leaving Jon and me standing there, dumbstruck.

"May I have your attention please? This is Major Lewis. I've replaced Col. Majors. We received word from Northern States Regional Commander General Scud heigh that we are to proceed north to his headquarters in Bismarck. Because it's too far away by land, he will send transport to Marshalltown, Iowa. We will be evacuated from there. I know some of you believe it's better to stay here on your own without government consent. I've decided that those of you who want to stay, can. But the general was very specific when he said the government will not support these holdouts. At 0600 tomorrow, we will load one semi with provisions and one tanker with fuel and fill the other two semis with people. If more want to leave, we can use another semi. We'll meet up with two other strongholds up there. Because I have relieved Col. Majors, I am now authorized to wear Major. That is all."

True to his word, at 0600 about 250 people were ready to leave the island. Over a hundred packed into each trailer, leaving us with barely 275. For the first time in months, we saw Col. Majors, and he was in horrible shape. He was swimming in his once proud uniform. He could barely make it to the trailer without collapsing.

We said our goodbyes to the convoy, not sure if we'd ever see them again. Each camp had tried to convince the other side to join them. Finally, the convoy boarded the barges. Of course Jon and I elected to remain, and once the others left, he and I were put in charge. We only had about seventy-five who could fight. Many of the others had decided to stay because they were too old to make the trek. The remainder were just too young. Five of the older guys had been in the army and were mechanics, and among our numbers was the dentist and two RNs.

It would be a long time before we ever learned that a week after the evacuees left, General Scudheigh ambushed and killed most of them and raped the women. Lewis, meanwhile, ate a bullet. Fucking Coward. Poetically, Scudheigh— or Jim Mathews, according to his birth certificate—met his gruesome end, not by zombies or the real army, but by getting his dick bit off by one of his sex slaves. Tragic to think that before all this he was a Little League coach.

Lewis didn't leave us with much. We had enough food and fuel for most of the winter, and we guessed we'd make it to April. We'd have to go out on foot for more semis and vehicles and only got two decent vehicles, then probably make two runs—one for weapons, ammo, and material for the wall, another for medicine, food, and more ammo. We were in good shape with fuel. Twenty-five of the young able bodied stayed behind and kept on the lookout. By then the wall ran from sector Four to Nine.

We boarded the barges in the only two vehicles we had. Our destination was a Lowe's about six miles inland, and next to Lowe's was a hunting outfitter. But first we had to get some semis. We left before dawn and headed south of the original landing zone by Case to a trucking company. The old warehouse that used to serve as a corporate office was a scene from a warzone. From the looks of it, we'd missed a royal shootout—by a few years. Most of the bodies showed that they had been killed by bullet wounds and not bitten. There had to be over 1,000 spent shell casings on the ground. The local national guard and police department had set up a roadblock and established a blockhouse in the warehouse, using the semis as funnels. But despite all their careful planning, something clearly went wrong. There were corpses of soldiers and cops everywhere. It was as if they'd suddenly stopped shooting the dead and started shooting each other. Since we were poorly armed ourselves, we checked around for weapons. Naturally they were all gone.

It was already noon, and most of the day had been wasted getting here. Jon and I decided we'd check out the trucking company and get a few trucks to fill with supplies. We went inside and were shocked by what we saw. Everywhere we looked we saw the remains of women, children, and the elderly, almost all with a single bullet hole in their skull. There was no way for us to tell if any had been bitten. Behind a lock door, in an upstairs storage room, we found an old colt revolver next to a headless skeleton. In his hands was a note that read, "Had to give up, tell Tracy and Michelle I'm sorry. National Guard turned on us when they realized we had no food. Cops tried to stop them. Overrun—nothing we could do. They left us with two pistols. I'm so sorry."

"Its good he was compassionate," Jon said, breaking the silence.

"Huh?" I grunted.

"Well, he knew they were done for. He could have bolted, like the guard, but he killed them."

"Are you sure?" I said." He could be saying he was sorry for giving up. He was behind a locked door. Why wouldn't he do it down there?"

"Well, guess we'll never know," Jon said as he picked up the rusty revolver. "How old do you think this is?"

"No clue," I answered.

"It's got one bullet in it. Must be my lucky day," he said, putting it in his coat pocket. We walked down to the maintenance garage and looked for truck keys. After a fruitless two-hour search, it was time to hotwire them. Luckily, one of the old-timers, Bruce Tuttle, who'd come with us knew how, and away we went in our procured semis. By now it was getting late, so we headed out to the landing zone and carefully pulled the trucks onto the barges.

The next morning, before we really had time to digest the previous day's non-events, the power went out on the island. The diesel generator had finally given up. It had been running for three years, with no real breaks. We'd never even thought about it breaking down. Jesse and Bill found a manual and said that maybe they could get it going again, but we needed a more reliable one for the winter. Sgt. Johnston said once upon a time you could rent them at most equipment rental places, so we pulled out the map and phone book. By now, we had developed a sophisticated system of marking where we'd been. On the building we would paint a circle with an X through it, and on the map the same symbol appeared on corresponding spot to the building. There were two rental places about six blocks and ten blocks from the Case plant.

Using what daylight we had, we scrounged some material to reinforce the semis to make them safer. The only machine guns we had left were in place at our defensive positions and couldn't be spared. It took three days, but finally the trucks were ready to go. But the generator was in bad shape and fall was rapidly approaching.

We developed a simple plan: we would take a tractor without a trailer, swing by the trucking company, pick up a flatbed, and proceed to the closest rental place. Meanwhile, Jon's group of three escorts—one Hummer and two Jeeps—and the other two semis would go to Lowe's and the gun shop. They would stop for nothing. While they were doing those tasks, I would take a Camaro, that was left abandoned nearby the Case plant, and check on that house we'd found. When we were done planning, I decided to use the remaining daylight and go to the water tower. I climbed up and sat there facing the river.

Almost like there's not a million bloodthirsty monsters out there," Buck said as he joined me.

"I'm sure it's closer to a couple billion," I replied.

"No—I meant over there," he said, pointing to the Illinois side of the river.

"Holy crap," I exclaimed as I looked around the other side. There really must have been close to a million. They were packed as far back as the eye could see. A few "brave" ones were trying to swim or float or walk across, but they'd invariably slip under and not be seen.

"Scary, huh?" Buck said.

"What?" I asked not sure what he meant.

"That the difference between us being alive and dead is 250 feet of river, a wall, and you."

"Me?" Now I really wasn't sure what he meant.

"Well, duh," he said.

"How so?"

"If you hadn't done what you did and gone and gotten things," he said, "we could have ended up like that trucking company."

"I hadn't thought of it like that. I was just trying to survive."

"Well, we all thank you. I don't know what we'd do without you and Jon."

"You're welcome, I guess. So what did you do before this?"

"Me? I was a simple lawyer. You know—chasing after ambulances until one day the hospitals started closing."

"Glad you didn't chase the wrong one, huh?"

"Oh yeah. It was a good thing I never went to the hospital. My sister was a nurse, and she said it was jammed full of assault victims. Seems like people were biting each other, and that's when she told me stay clear of the hospital. That was the last time I talked to her. I hope she took her own advice, but she lived to help people."

"I'm sure she made it."

"Thanks. But, you don't have to say that. I know she's gone. They're gone. What about you?"

"Ha! Would you believe I worked in a grocery store?"

"Nope. I'm just gonna pretend that before this you were a soldier."

"I guess I see your logic," I said.

Buck said his goodbyes and climbed back down the ladder, but I was in no hurry. I just couldn't believe it was that bad, but it was. I smacked the tank with my hand, and I was stunned to hear a hollow thud. Preoccupied as we were about scrounging food and ammo, we'd forgotten about the most important thing—water. I climbed to the hatch and looked in—about a quarter full.

I climbed down to the ground and found one of the mechanics. I asked him why our water would be so low. He explained that the island had a water purification facility, and since we lost power it wasn't pumping any. Besides that, the guy who'd been in charge had gone to Bismarck with his family—they'd lived up there—and without power or an operator, the plant shutdown.

"Do you know how it works?" I asked.

"Not really. There must be an operator manual up there. I kept meaning to ask you about it."

"You want the job?"

"Uh, I have my hands full fixing things. I was gonna suggest one of the older couples."

"Sounds good. Pick one and help them out if they need it." And just like that, I'd taken care of another problem. Maybe I was cut out for leadership role after all. I decided to hit the sack, because in about five hours we were going to roll out.

CHAPTER 4

Early the next morning, we had to rely on headlights when we assembled since we still had limited power. The different teams went to the tug by groups. The generator group, led by the two mechanics, went first. I went next, then Jon led the building supplies group. The tug cast off and we began our short south. Once we docked, each group gave a nod and took off for their different areas.

I loaded the shotgun and set it on the front seat of the Camaro, then took off for the house. After driving for about three minutes, I found it and saw there was only one pathetic zombie outside. Missing both legs, she was slowly crawling away from the house. When she realized I was there, she shifted her weight and started crawling toward me. I picked up a two by four from the ground and hit her in the head, and she stopped moving.

"Hello?" I called out as I walked toward the house. Nervous now. I decided to go around back, and when I turned the corner, my stomach dropped. The side door had been torn off. As I got closer, I saw it looked like it had been blown off from the outside.

"That's far enough—turn around real slow," said a voice from behind me. Parked next to my car were two large trucks with about ten guys.

"Now put down the gun," the man said. "They said you'd come back. I didn't believe them, but sure enough, ya did."

"What do you want?" I asked.

"We've seen you and your island, and it ain't fair. You keep raiding our town. We still own it and you got to pay your dues, Son."

"Which are?"

"You and your people, leave and give it to us," he said, approaching me with his gun raised.

"Seriously? It'll never happen, but you can live with us."

"This ain't a negotiation."

"Then just shoot me."

"In due time. We've fought hard to keep this place safe, and you keep tearing it up with your semis as you steal right from under our noses."

"You'd do the same if you were in our shoes."

"This isn't about me—it's about you," he said.

"Did you do this?" I asked, nodding toward the house.

"Of course I did. We killed all the zombies, and they refused to pay for our services."

"Pay?"

"It gets lonely being the military governor of Moline—if you catch my drift."

"We would have let you live with us on the island."

"Why live on a cramped island when I have all this land?"

"So you don't want our island?"

"The exact opposite. I don't want your kind to come onto my territory ever again."

"We can't do that—we need food too."

"Tough shit. Hope your guys know how to farm."

"You can kill me now, but we'll continue to search for food."

"Naturally, and when they stumble into our many traps, they'll suffer the consequences—just like you," he said as he lowered his pistol. Surely he wasn't going to shoot me—he was out of effective range. I was mistaken. He fired three quick shots, the first tearing into my left shoulder. The adrenaline hit me and I took off running behind the house, a hail of bullets chasing me. In my haste, I'd left my shotgun on the ground. Worse, they were surrounding my car—and my radio. When I heard one truck take off; I figured they were trying to flush me out. I ran as fast as I could toward the other houses, cutting into the alley and looking over my shoulder. Nothing yet. *Where am I gonna run to?* I knew I had to get away. As I neared the street, I heard the truck as it pulled up into the alley about three houses from the end. I cut back between two houses onto the main street. I looked to where my car was parked, and it was gone. Great—now I had to outrun *three* cars. I crossed the main street still at a full sprint. I slid underneath a wooden fence and climbed up into a dilapidated tree house. I sat there catching my breath as both trucks doubled back and stopped next each other on the street. Men started getting out of the trucks.

"We know you can hear us!" one of them yelled. "Just give up and we'll make it quick. If you stay out here in the dark and bleeding, one of the roamers will get you. And then you'll be one of them. Is that what you want?" After what seemed like forever, one truck took off. Now four others disembarked from the other truck, two heading for the end of the block while the other two headed the opposite way. One lone guy sat in the bed watching, for me. I knew they'd find me eventually, and since I was trapped, I was almost out of time. I sat there and watched as the men walked down behind me and wandered back to the truck. They yelled and hollered, trying to goad me to come out. Then they started their truck and took off.

I looked down at my arm. My sleeve was soaked in blood, and I was getting shocky. I knew the tug would take off in about an hour, so I got down out of the tree and started cutting between houses. It took me maybe thirty minutes to cover four blocks. I had three to go, and I doubted I'd make it. My wound was slowing me down.

I finally reached a four-lane road and was about to cross when I saw cars coming. When I jumped back into the ditch, I landed on my shoulder and screamed out in pain. I peered back up and thought I'd lost my mind because there was Jon's convoy. With the last of my strength, I stood up and started chasing after them. Luckily, someone looked back and saw me, and the trailing vehicle's brake lights gave me a new-found strength. I took off at a sprint, and when I caught up, the right-hand back door opened and a familiar figure popped out and grabbed me as I collapsed. I passed out in the back seat of the Jeep as they took off my shirt.

When I awoke on the tug, Jon asked me what happened. I didn't respond—I went back to sleep. I woke up a few days later in the base clinic. When I tried to move my head, I found it was strapped down, as was the rest of me.

Jon was right there. "We had to be safe," he said.

"I understand, but I was shot."

"We figured that much out. It was straight through the meaty part of your shoulder. You're lucky. The dentist patched you up."

"Well, I did have help," Doc said, meaning the nurses, "but you need to stay in bed for a few more days. You lost a lot of blood, and to be honest, you should be dead. We didn't know what type of blood you were, and we had very little O." I thanked him and the nurses.

Jon told me that while I was out he'd learned what happened and had wanted to take a little revenge. Then we talked about another run. "I was thinking that maybe we need some entertainment," he said.

"What'd you have in mind?"

"Swing by Best Buy, pick up iPods, TVs, Xboxes, ya know?"

"What's brought this on?"

"We're too stressed—we gotta slow down."

The next day, three more semis loaded up with no problem. When Jon woke me up, he was wearing the biggest grin I'd ever seen on his face.

"What's going on?" I said.

"You'll die when you see them."

"See what?" He took me out to show me, and I was shocked to see three sixty-inch TVs being installed in the mess hall.

"Holy shit."

"So what do you think?"

"Are we putting them in the mess hall?"

"Um . . . I don't think they'll fit."

"Huh?"

"I wasn't showing you the TVs—I was showing you those babies." He pointed to three armored troop transports.

"Can I ask how and why?"

"The 'why' is because, as you proved, we'll need them. As long as there are humans out there, we'll get shot at." Then he explained how they found them. They were pulling up to Best Buy, right down the block from Wal-Mart. As they approached the off-ramp to Coal Valley, they noticed that there were a line of cars that had been blocked. They took one of the vehicles to see what was up, and to their amazement there sat the three troop transports and a tank—all out of gas. The transports took diesel, but the tank took a higher-grade mix. To be on the safe side, they took a grenade from the transport and dropped it in the tank. They figured that if anyone ever got it running, it could do us some serious damage.

"So other than that, anything happen?"

"While we were going down I-74, someone took a shot at us."

"And?"

"Kept on going. It was way off."

"Good."

The next two weeks flew by, and I was finally good to go for the last supply run for the winter. One thing we needed to find this run was a parts for a windmill. Jesse said he thought he could build one. It was worth a shot because the fuel we saved generating electricity with wind would be used for our vehicles. Even after the world ended, we still depended on fuel.

The morning of the run, Jon came up to me and said we should take one of the transports. I agreed. We loaded everyone into two of them. It had twin machine guns and had the same top speed as the semis. Doc and the mechanics gave us their lists, and the people in charge of food told us what they needed. Everything could fit into two semis, but we took three just to be safe. Our trip would take us through to East Moline—virgin territory for us. Once ashore, we covered the fifteen blocks to another Super Wal-Mart. It'd been awhile since we'd seen any zombies.

As we approached the deserted parking lot, we saw that the Wal-Mart had burned down. We got out and discussed where to go. Across the street were a Jewel-Osco and a Walgreens—they'd have the food and meds we needed. We went across and loaded up one semi about three-quarters full, then headed for Lowe's, where we figured we'd get the parts the mechanics needed. When we got there, we found what we needed, including twelve boxes of six-foot windmills and the electrical components on the list. We loaded everything into the semi and took off.

We were flying down I-74. When we made our turn toward the tug the shit hit the fan. We got a message from Bruce Tuttle, the tug captain saying he was under attack by six motorcycles and two trucks. They'd blocked the ramp and were peppering the boat with lead. Jon, in the lead transport, said to catch up to him—he'd go ahead and clear a path. We took over his position as he jumped onto one of the .50 cals. His driver stopped the lumbering vehicle, and fourteen guys got out and piled into ours. Then Jon sped ahead, and by the time we got to the dock the carnage was over. It looked as if Jon's driver had smashed into one of the pickups and then flipped onto its side. We slowed up as the semis raced by and loaded onto the approaching tug. We saw Jon crouched behind the transport, firing at the remaining truck. Both gunners unloaded on the enemy. A second later, the gunner on the right fell down into the cab, bleeding from his back.

"Behind us," yelled the other gunner, Sgt. Harris. I quickly told one of the other guys to man the gun. From the passenger side I used the periscope to direct the driver into position between Jon and the gunfire. The gunners were blasting away at the trap. Meanwhile, the semis started getting onto the tug. There were shots ringing out from all sides of the dock. Through the periscope I spotted a guy launching an RPG. Luckily one of the gunners saw him too, and it veered wide.

Jon crawled into the back of the armored vehicle covered in blood and mud. He said they were waiting for them. They put tire spikes down, causing the transport to flip, killing everyone else. He got lucky when he was tossed out, but he thought he'd dislocated his shoulder. We backed the transport to the wreck, opened the back hatches, and removed all the salvageable equipment. Another RPG raced by the last semi being loaded onto the barge. The tug captain said we need to mount up, so we finished gathering the ammo and guns from the wreck and started back to the dock, but we were stuck in the mud. When they saw us make our retreat, the assailants decided to make a break for the tug. About seven motorcycles and ten men on foot took off running, leaving a few to take shots at us. The .50 cals on the transport open fired but had a hard time hitting the bikes. The runners, however, weren't so lucky. A couple more RPGs whizzed by, missing. Those guys were horrible shots. The .50 cals homed in on where they thought they were coming from.

Meanwhile, four motorcycles made it to the tug. A fifth biker flipped and was pinned between his bike and the second semi. The guys who made it to the tug hid behind the semi furthest back and were firing at the pilot house, so the captain radioed he was pulling back. The transport finally broke free of the mud, and when it got to the ramp the remaining group broke off the engagement. We had six guys trapped in the corner of the barge. Two of them tried to jump over the side and were shot by two men on the bridge. The other four, seeing their brothers die, knew all hope was lost, so they charged down the side of the barge toward the pilot house. Sitting ducks without cover, they were quickly killed. Johnston, in the bridge, was hit by a wild shot, but it was a flesh wound and he was okay. The biker who was pinned pleaded with us to kill him, but cool heads prevailed and we tied him up and dragged him to our "jail" in spite of his injuries. It had actually been a jail at one time, but we'd been using as an office even though it couldn't be unlocked from the inside and had no windows.

That night we had a meeting during dinner to discuss what to do with him. Everyone was against letting him go. The wives of two of the men killed wanted his blood, and they weren't alone—about half of the others felt the same. We'd planned to question him after the memorial for the four we lost that day. It was about 10:30 when Jon and I went to talk to him. Doc, who was there with two guards, said his leg was pretty bad, but he should be okay in a few weeks. He'd given him some painkillers, so he was out for the night.

We went back to the jail to grill him the next day. "What do you want?" he said sourly.

"We want to talk," Jon said.

"So talk," the man said.

"Do you have a name?" I asked.

"Yep."

"Which is?" I asked, impatient.

"Not telling ya. I want my lawyer."

"Seriously?" Jon said sarcastically.

"Yep. And my phone call."

"You think this is fucking funny?" Jon said angrily.

"You're all dead, might as well give up," he said.

"Why's that?" I asked.

"You'll see," he said, and it went on like that for almost thirty minutes. Finally we gave up.

Jon, myself and a few others were making plans for the upcoming winter—and it we determined it was going to be a busy one. The third and fourth generators were up and running, as the first and second had been completed the week previously. We were finishing dinner and walking back to our rooms, as darkness fell when we saw headlights up on the bridge. They stopped up there, then quickly went out. Jon and I took off running to the command center. It had been at least a year since the siren had sounded for an actual emergency. We turned on the PA Jon announced, "All regulars soldiers and armed men report to the command center. All rovers man your stations. All non-defense personnel report to the gym—now! This is not a drill! I say again, *this is not a drill!*" Within a few minutes, we had fifty-five men standing by in the command center. We armed everyone and sent five men to the gym to stand guard there led by Harris. We sent Simpson and Black to secure the generator station and to turn off all outside floodlights. As they flickered out, we heard a thundering boom.

CHAPTER 5

"What the hell was that?" a voice squawked over the radio.

"Turn on the lights back on," Jon said calmly into the radio. When the floodlights kicked back on, we climbed to the roof of the building and looked around, and a few moments later we spotted a giant boulder at the edge of the darkness. We climbed down to a Hummer parked there, got in, and headed toward the boulder. One of the younger kids, Simon, in the water tower said over the radio, "They're up to something. There are lights on up there, but we can't make out what they're doing." The six of us in the Hummer all had a bad feeling.

"You're not gonna believe this, but looks like they're using the boulder as a zip line," Jon said.

"Zip line?" a voice said from behind me.

"Like a cable slide," I explained quickly, then into the radio, I said, "Get everyone ready to defend, armed to the teeth. We'll approach from the south side."

"Got it. We'll forma defensive perimeter around the north end of Main Street," Jon said. We pulled up to the boulder and illuminated it with our high beams. A few seconds later, the Sector Eight patrol moved just south of the boulder. Meanwhile, the patrol from Sector Nine joined up with us.

"There's movement," a hushed tone said over the radio.

"Can you get a count?" Jon asked.

"I see maybe five. Oh shit, they're headed toward us," the voice said. A few tense seconds passed, then about a dozen shots rang.

A shout pierced the air. "Zombies!"

"Ted's been bit. I dropped my ammo. I think there's six left. I'm running toward Sector Eight," a frightened voice said.

The shift commander's voice boomed over the PA. "There are zombies inside the walls—I repeat, there are zombies inside the walls. If you aren't at the gym, get there now. I repeat—this is not a drill. Remain calm—we have plans for this."

"Give me a count, gym," the shift commander asked, following procedure.

"We have all but six—all but the family who oversees the water supply. We're locking the doors," the guard in charge of the gym, Brandon Williams, replied.

"We locked ourselves in the main tank," came a woman's voice. "There's me, my husband, our two kids, my niece, and sister-in-law."

"All personnel accounted for then," Brandon said.

"Copy that," the shift commander said. "Strike team, base. Report position." Our military training was intact.

"Base, strike team. We're about thirty feet south of the rock. No movement. Where are the floodlights?" the man next to me said.

"They're not coming back on. The breaker is tripped and won't reset. We've got a portable one coming to you now," the shift commander said.

"Copy that," I said.

"All patrols, check in." The shift commander was still going down his checklist. Patrols one and three through seven checked in. I assumed two was the patrol from Sector Eight. We heard a car pull up behind us and stop, and Jesse and Ryan hopped out. The mechanic fumbled with a portable floodlight and turned it on. The boulder and area behind it was a ghastly sight, yet still no movement. The patrol from nine drove up on their golf cart.

"Base, strike team. Still no movement," a voice on the radio said.

"Copy."

The mechanic took off while Ryan stayed to help out. We broke into two teams, four on the right, four on the left, with Ryan in the Hummer following slowly. Lighting the way as we cautiously approached the boulder. We were hit by the familiar stench of rotting flesh as we fanned out and formed a semicircle around the huge rock. The Hummer stopped, and in its headlights we saw a half-severed zombie struggling to move. It was a teenage boy, and lying next to him was a meat hook that had been used to travel down the zip line. I explained that to Jon that they had shot the boulder across with a zip line attached to, presumably, the bridge and then the zombies were slid across. Then someone on the bridge cut the line so that the zombies would simply drop down with ease or so we couldn't get off. Either way, the line was just lying on the ground.

"Now what?" I asked Jon.

"We're going to form a perimeter across the island stretching from Sector Seven to Eleven," Jon replied over his radio.

"What do you want me to do?"

"Start in Ten and work your way to Nine, then when you clear Ten proceed to Seven and Eight. We'll start walking north to close the gap. We have two floodlights on each transport. Gym and water plant, keep everyone inside and double-check that windows and doors are locked, and put two people on the gym roof."

"Copy," Brandon said.

"Understood," the woman from the water plant said.

We got to the first row of houses in Sector Ten. We lived in the houses closest to the center of the island, so most of these houses were deserted. No one wanted to be the first line of defense. We searched each house, and after about six hours, we declared ten all clear. In that time, there had been no zombie attacks on the line, nor had we heard from the "missing patrol." The island wasn't that big, so we were getting nervous that the zombies had somehow given us the slip.

"Change of plans," Jon said, breaking the silence. "Since we know they aren't in the houses and you've cleared all 160 of them, we're sending over six guys to watch the houses. Once they get there, go to the boulder and track the zombies. We'll continue advancing north. Gym—any visuals? Also, I sent two guys to the tower. Tower—any visuals?"

"Sorry, nothing," the gym guard said.

"Nothing," Simon, the guy in the tower said as our relief arrived. We headed to the boulder.

"Base, gym. The people are getting restless. They want to know what's happening," the gym guard said.

"Tell them everything," Jon said.

"Understood," Brandon said. We were back at the boulder now and starting to look around. We headed to where we expected to find a dead guard and found a lot of blood on the tall grass. We caught a break when we spotted a small blood trail that headed northeast. We followed it for about ten minutes, and that's when we saw the invaders. They had encircled one of the old towers used in the very early days of the outbreak. A ladder was lying on the ground.

"I think we found them," I said into the radio.

"Where?" Jon said.

"Um, Tower Nine-One."

"We're at least twelve hours away at this pace," Jon said.

"We'll proceed with caution." From about fifty yards away, we lined up to take a shot at a different target.

"Now," I yelled. Instantly four of the ten dropped, a fifth lost his balance, by tripping over one of the fallen zombies and started toward us, and three more gave up trying to get into the tower and started toward us.

"Hold your ground—let them get closer," I said. A tense minute passed. "Now!" I said, and all five dropped in unison. We crept behind the remaining two and let them have it.

As one of the guards went to pick up the ladder, another zombie fell from the tower behind him and landed with a bone crunching splat. We yelled at the guard when it started to get up, and he quickly got out of the line of fire. Two of the eleven fallen zombies turned out to be former guards. Obviously, the zombie who'd fallen from the tower was one. We found his radio a few hours later by an overturned golf cart.

I was starving, and so was everyone else. Some went to the mess hall and grabbed a portable grill to take to the gym. It was going to be a lot longer to clear out the zombies than we figured. We made ourselves some sandwiches, using our horrible wheat bread, for a midnight snack. After we ate, we joined up with the line and moved ever so slowly north until we got to the coast. We counted the bodies—still twelve. Jon said a few words about God and eternal heaven. We then released the people from their various hiding spots and ate a super-late lunch.

No one was allowed to go north of Zone A, but we were pretty sure all the zombies had been eliminated. After almost two days of searching for zombies, the sun was finally setting, and we gave the all clear. On the way home, we were stopped by several men outside the jail demanding justice, in the mood for a hanging. We talked the crowd down and added three more guards to watch over the captive.

Immediately after breakfast the next morning, we held another town meeting. It was unanimous: We were at war with the people on the land, and this man was our prize. We would form committees of the older people, and some of the young would be trained as home guards, with previous guards being tasked with offensive weapons, to better defend and protect ourselves from the growing threat. After the meeting, Jon and I went to interrogate the prisoner.

"How'd ya sleep?" Jon asked the prisoner.

"Like a baby. You?" he replied hoarsely.

"Like a bug in a rug," Jon said.

"Really. Sounds like you guys were up late. It's not gonna stop, ya know? They are going to keep this up until you are destroyed."

"We fully understand, but it's time for you to talk."

"Yeah—ain't gonna happen. Might as well kill me."

"Don't tempt me."

We brought Doc in. He had some smelling salts and a few filled needles. "Something to dull the pain," he said as he gave him a shot, which was an overdose of morphine. He whispered, "You tried to kill my six-year-old son. I feel no sympathy for you." Within minutes, the prisoner was out like a light. We hung him from the ceiling by his handcuffs, then placed a belt around his injured leg. Doc then woke him up with smelling salts.

"What's up, bitches?" the prisoner said groggily, looking around.

"In my past life, I'd numb him with Novocain and pull out his teeth," Doc said.

"Well, in my past life, I took care of them," the prisoner said, more alert now. Jon grabbed him by the neck, put two fingers in his nostrils, and pulled back his head. I grabbed his jaw while Doc inserted a sinister-looking device used to prop open a patient's mouth. The man struggled at first, but he quickly tired because of the drugs and the lack of food. Doc focused on the healthiest tooth he saw and probed around with an instrument. Then he got hold of it with his dental pliers and gave a yank. The man screamed in pain, aware that his life was going to end painfully.

"Still a tough guy?" Jon said into the man's ear. His mouth full and unable to spit, he looked away as his eyes started tearing up. "I'll take that as a 'yes.' Doctor, please proceed."

Doc cleared away the rubble of the prisoner's canine tooth, exposing a bare socket. Then he grabbed a bottle of peroxide. "Over-the-counter peroxide is three percent. This is sixteen. Thirty percent is lethal, so we'll be okay." Doc measured a capful, and the man tried to turn away, causing doc to spill the liquid. The man looked relieved, but while his guard was down, Doc poured peroxide into his mouth right from the bottle. The wound started to foam, and the prisoner screamed in agony as he tried to push his tongue into the wound. After he stopped thrashing, Doc gave him a small glass of water, which he quickly swished around.

"I'll make you a deal," Jon said. "You give us the location of the rest of your people, and we'll let you live out your days on the island a few meters south of us. We'll give you food to plant and some building materials. We'll let you heal, because the people on this island want blood. The people you used to live with will know it was you who sold them out. But more importantly, the small island is safe from zombies." Jon then pulled the device out from the mouth.

"I can't," the man said dejectedly.

"Why the hell not?" Jon roared back.

"He'll kill my kids."

"How do I know you're telling the truth?"

"In my pants is a picture from four years ago. That's how he makes us do things—by threatening to kill or rape our families."

"Why don't you fight back?"

"You know Richard Mooney, from the news? He used his celebrity status to become the leader, because people thought he knew what to do. But he's crazy. He has people brainwashed. He has them eating out of his hand."

"Well, give us the location of your fort and we'll put a stop to him."

"I can't."

"Then we continue. Doc?" he said, nodding at the doctor.

"Well, I may have an idea," Doc said.

"About what?" Jon said, turning around.

"Well, I've been thinking. What're we going to do when we know the location?"

"We hadn't gotten that far."

"I know, but follow me. I think I know of a way out of this sticky situation." Doc obviously didn't want the prisoner to hear what he had to say, so we followed him out of the room. As he shut the door, he said, "I'm not saying this will work, but my former partner had a floatplane."

"Floatplane? Like the kind that land on water?" I asked.

"Exactly, only his had wheels too. So why can't we make an observation flight and find their base that way?" Doc said.

"Who would fly it? Because we can't afford to lose you, Doc. Pass the word that we're looking for a pilot," Jon said.

"Aren't we rushing this? How do we know the plane is still at your partner's house" I asked.

"Because he was in Seattle at the outbreak, visiting his mother. He called me before the city was locked down and told me he'd be back ASAP. Obviously, he didn't make it," Doc explained.

"They tried to level Seattle, didn't they?" I asked.

"Yeah. The air force came in and napalmed it. Everything was burned to a crisp, but it didn't stop them," Jon.

"So we should stop torturing him?" I asked.

"Yes, because I have a backup plan. We can put a tracking chip in his leg wound."

"Ah. Where are we going to get one? And how are we gonna get him to do that?" Jon asked.

"I don't know. I'm just saying that if I was in his shoes, I'd hold out for as long as I could to buy my family time. Listen—I'm going to go check on him."

"Remote control helicopter with a camera!" Jon said suddenly.

"What?" I said, confused.

"You know—the toy? We could follow with that over-head." Jon explained.

"Ain't gonna work—he'll hear it."

"So what do you have in mind, oh wise one?" Jon said sarcastically.

"I don't know, but I do know that we've got to protect our north end, so we don't have to do a daily island sweep. We got lucky we saw them when we did."

"Do you have any ideas?"

"One. That kid—Simon."

"The one who can hit a zombie in the eye from a ridiculous distance and the one that talks to that dog of his like it's a person?"

"Yep."

"Okay?"

"We can take him out to the support column in a rowboat and he can take potshots at them."

"Two problems. Are we going to find any volunteers to take him out, and is he going to leave that dog of his?"

"I don't know about either of those things, Jon. I'm just winging it," I said.

Doc returned and said, "He's doing fine."

"Considering his situation, he won't say anything. So just lock him up in the closet. Maybe he'll crack," Jon said.

"Doc can handle that," I said.

Doc nodded, then said, "Well, I feel bad for the guy, but I think I've got a recording of the zombies feeding." That caught me and Jon off guard.

"What the fuck?" Jon exclaimed.

"Well, I never did tell anyone what happened to my wife."

"I understand. That's rough, Doc," Jon said.

"I just take solace knowing she's not one of them."

"How do you know that?" Jon said.

"True love just knows," Doc said, fighting back a tear.

"Doc, you're out there," I said, trying to lighten the mood.

"We all are, to still be alive," he responded.

We went to the back room, grabbed the half-dead prisoner, and stuck him in a closet. We tied his hands behind his back, then stuffed towels under the door. We wanted everyone to keep quiet when near the closet, including the guards. We told them to keep him alive, hoping he'd snap. We then let the rumor mill run its course. Everyone assumed we killed him. The guards knew, but they knew that not knowing what some maniac was doing to your kids was torture enough.

CHAPTER 6

The next day we met with Doc after he'd checked to see how the prisoner was doing. "He finally gave up something—his name's Tom," Doc said. "I explained to him that the longer they know he's alive hereon the island, the more likely it is they're going to harm his family. But I don't think he's going to budge."

"Didn't expect him to. So where's this plane you mentioned?" Jon said.

"Right there," Doc said, pointing to a house on the Rock River on the map.

"Okay—seems easy enough," I said.

"I gotta run and check on everyone else," Doc said.

When Doc was gone, I said, "Our best option is to go get the plane, bring it to the airport, just south of us, then take it up for a little recon."

"Why is that the best option?"

"Because that's how we're going to find them."

"Oh. Is that because they have a giant sign on the roof?"

"No, although, that would help. Tom will be more likely to open up if he thinks we found them on our own and are going to demolish their place."

"And because they'll have seen our plane and assume that's how we found their hideout. And maybe it will keep his family from getting punished by Mooney."

"Precisely." We'd told only ten other people about the plane, and Doc had found a woman, Susan, who'd flown commercial planes in the late '80s. The downside was that she was about sixty-five, but she'd said she could handle it. As a backup, she'd agreed to teach someone younger to fly the plane when she returned.

The initial mission was to get the plane. For the first time, we wore body armor and helmets. Jon and I rode in the compartment of the armored vehicle next to five other men, two gunners, the driver, and Susan. This was the farthest inland we'd be going onto land. It would be a drive of about four

49

miles straight across, but with all the avoidance of zombies it would be more like ten miles.

As we disembarked the barge, we made sure the captain understood that he was to go back to the island, and when we were coming back, we'd call him when we were twenty minutes from the ramp so he could meet us as we were pulling up.

After thirty minutes of back-road driving, we finally made it to the junction of I-74 and I-280. It was a mess of burned-out wrecks. Once we got onto the highway, we had to drive on the grassy median. To our left was the airport, and we saw maybe 2,000 cattle grazing in the field there.

"I'd kill for some real meat," Susan said, breaking the silence. We all nodded.

"Wonder how we'd get those onto the island," Jon whispered in my ear.

"Focus. But I already thought about it. There's plenty of grass at the ends of the island. Plane first, though." We got off the interstate after another twenty-five minutes on the median, and then it took almost four hours to weave the behemoth around abandoned vehicles on the narrow roads. We finally got to the site on the Rock Rivera little after two p.m. When we determined the plane could carry just four people, we left Jon, Susan, and a younger guy, named Garrett, there. We didn't want to still be on the road in the dark, so the rest of us piled back into the transporter and headed back to meet the tug and got there without a hitch.

To Jon's utter frustration, they couldn't find the keys to the plane. No one had thought of that. He called Doc over the radio. "Doc, you there?" Jon said.

"Yeah, what's up?" Doc replied.

"Do you know where the keys to the plane are?"

Doc thought for a moment, then said, "They should be inside the house, on the hook right by the kitchen door, attached to a yellow thing that floats."

Jon looked, and after a minute, he said angrily, "Not there. Looks like we'll be camping here tonight." The others joined him inside the house.

"Jon, wait," Doc said in a panic. "His teenage son was in town. So something might be there." Just as Doc said that, a horribly disfigured teenage boy appeared in the shadows. Jon shot at him, but Garrett didn't turn around in time—or he thought he was the target. Either way, he was shot in the arm and fell over a chair. Before he had a chance to scream, a second figure emerged and bit down on his throat. Jon fired several times and hit all three in the head.

"Doc, there was a teenage girl in here. She's blonde and wearing panties."

"No idea—maybe a girlfriend."

"Either way, I had to put the kid down," Jon said.

"Fuck. I'll tell his folks."

Jon searched the house for the keys, then called Doc again. "I still can't find the keys."

"Try the kid's room."

"I already looked there," Jon said, frustrated.

"The plane?"

"I thought you said the house."

"I don't know for sure," Doc said defensively.

"We'll look again." It was starting to get dark, and Jon and the pilot quickly walked over to the river plane. They didn't find any keys.

{extra space}

"How far are you guys?" Jon asked me when he got me on the radio.

"Just radioed the tug," I said.

"Well at first light, we'll need a ride."

"We can turn back if you want."

"No, I'll be fine."

The tug pulled up as we reached the ramp and the sun began to set as we loaded up. "Good timing," I said to the tugboat captain, who just nodded.

"We got movement on the bridge," Simon said excitedly. What he saw was a catapult riding in the bed of a pickup truck. Another truck had two large rocks in them. The third truck had several zombies attached to a cable and, he saw all of this from on top of one of the column supporting the bridge. "What do you want me to do?" he asked excitedly.

"You know what to do," I said to him. "We'll be there as soon as the tug casts off. Doc, turn on all the floodlights, point them at the bridge. Get everyone to the gym, including the guards and rovers. Keep a small group in the security center and go to the gym to keep people calm."

"And our guest?" Doc said via the radio.

"Leave him in the closet, tell the guards to leave, and once the crisis is over to head back."

"I'm opening fire now," Simon said, more relaxed. As the tug chugged toward the island, I thought back to when we first approached Simon about the lookout task and asking about his golden retriever, Skip. Simon had lived on a farm with his grandparents, and he'd had Skip since he was a boy of twelve. He told of the day when three zombies cornered him in his barn, and Skip came out of nowhere and tripped the first zombie and knocked over another. As the zombie struggled with Skip, Simon grabbed a pitch fork and drove it straight through its head. Simon and Skip made their way to the island with others fleeing the zombies, when he heard Col. Major was opening up the island up. Since then he thanks Skip every morning for saving him.

I was quickly snapped back to the present with Simon's first shot, which hit the driver of the lead truck in the chest. Before the passenger could react, Simon nailed him too. They started firing blindly at the newly built barricade of cars, to prevent crossing of the bridge, not once firing up into the top of the bridge. Once Simon realized they had no idea where he was, he shot a third member in the arm.

"I count six more guys and what looks to be a dozen zombies," Simon said quickly. The wounded man fell to the ground in front of the small group of zombies. As soon as he got up, Simon put him right back down with a shot in the back. It was at that moment the attackers realized Simon was above them and sought cover behind the lead truck. Meanwhile, the third truck was rocking as the zombies in the bed of the truck were trying to get free of the cable that imprisoned them.

"I've got no clear shot," Simon said. "I'm going to aim for the wire." He fired and missed, catching one of the soulless creatures in the leg. The next shot missed completely. "They're moving below me now." He watched as they took turns covering each other so they could make their way to the ladder to his perch. There was a clearing of maybe twenty-five yards before the barricade. As the first target started sprinting and his buddies opened fire, Simon crawled forward, dodging bullets. *Finally—a moving target*, he thought. He lined up his shot and nailed him. The man took a few more steps and dropped.

Seeing his buddy hit the ground, one of his compatriots took off through the clearing. He was quickly followed by another. They approached the area where the first guy had been. Simon got the lead runner in his sights and quickly fired, unsure if the bullet had found its mark. Simon's spotter yelled, "Got him." The other runner was still on the loose, and Simon had time for one quick shot. His bullet hit mere inches from the man's foot, causing him to stumble to the ground. Before he could get up, Simon finished him off.

Seeing their buddies mowed down was enough for the rest of the raiding party. But when they turned around, they were shocked to see their former weapons on the loose. Trapped, they fired at the zombies and quickly dispatched them. Then they had to sprint across open ground again to get to their vehicles. The remaining three sprinted to the lead truck. Simon took his time and hit the middle runner in the back of the shoulder, causing him to twist and stumble. The same bullet plowed through and hit the lead runner in the leg. The last runner was behind the lead truck, yelling to his buddies. The one with the wounded leg was trying to put pressure on his leg when Simon put another round in his other calf. The one with the shoulder wound tried to play possum. The last guy had had enough. He ducked into the third truck and backed away. Simon fired three quick shots, the first hitting the roof of the cab, the second hitting the windshield just to the right of the driver, and the third hitting the hood.

"One got away," he said, pissed.

"We're here now to assist you, Simon," I said, irritated that I'd missed another fight. "Grab the two wounded guys." We climbed up the ladder as Simon and his spotter, Ryan, climbed down to survey their work. "They'll be back," I said to Simon.

"I know. I hope so," Simon said enthusiastically. Ryan climbed down to the rowboat and went to get more supplies for their continuing stake out on the top of the bridge.

We took our two new captives to the jail and separated them. Doc checked them over and said they'd be just fine. We left them in their pain in their new homes.

"Everything kosher, Jon?" I radioed.

"Well it's no Hilton, but it sure beats your mom's bed. We've cleared the house and locked ourselves in the attic. It's cold up here, but it could be worse."

"You want me to stay on the line and keep you company?" I asked.

"Nah—you guys have to get up early to be here by first light."

Four hours later someone woke me to tell me Jon was calling. I dressed quickly and headed over to the command center. "What's up, Jon?" I said.

"We got company," he said very quietly.

"What kind?"

"The neighborhood welcoming committee."

"Zombies?"

"Right."

"So?"

"So there's more than we can handle."

"What do you mean?"

"It's like they know we're here."

"Is that possible?"

"I don't know. If you told me two years ago that I'd be surrounded by them, I'd say you were crazy, but now—"

"Okay—we can be there in about five hours."

"Not in the dark, you can't."

"So what do you want me to do?"

"I wanted to alert you."

"Okay—we'll assemble in an hour, be on the road in about three."

"Copy."

"Good luck."

"Thanks—you too."

Hours later we at Jon's location and quickly overpowered close to a hundred zombies. We went into the house but found no sign of Jon Susan.

"Where are you?" I asked Jon over the radio.

"In the plane," Jon responded.

"Asshole. Do you know we are where you were?"

"Sorry—we hotwired it."

"Seriously?"

"Kidding. We checked the boy—the keys were in his pants. I assume he and his zombie lady-friend were gonna get the hell out of dodge, before they turned."

"And you didn't call why?"

"We've been trying. I think these things don't work too well in the air."

"All right—we're going to head back then."

"Sweet—we'll follow you in the air." It was then we saw the bright yellow plane swoop down. "We can cruise around today looking for them, and cover your retreat while we're at it."

"You do realize we wouldn't be here if it wasn't for you."

"I know, I know." We loaded up food and other odds and ends from the house and garage and headed back to the interstate. After three hours, we were almost to the loading dock.

"You've got company," Jon said.

"Where?"

"Two trucks running parallel to you on the next street to your right." I looked and couldn't see anything; both gunners had their eyes fixed that way.

"What the fuck is that?" the driver said to me. "The road ahead is blocked by a train."

"Jon, what is going on?"

"What do you mean?"

"There's a fucking train blocking the road ahead."

"It appears someone wants you to stop."

"Thanks. Sarcasm isn't appreciated right now, fuck-stick." I told the gunners to get ready and we turned right. The two trucks tried to intercept us with rockets, but none hit their mark and our gunners reduced them to ribbons.

"I think we pissed them off," I said.

"Oh yes—you did, all right."

"What?"

"You've got a barricade about four blocks to your left"— the road leading to the docks.

"I need an exit," I said.

"We got ya," John said

As we passed the barricades, both gunners opened up, but we wouldn't smash through the cement road dividers they'd set up. We headed away, then sat for twenty-five minutes while Jon circled, looking for a way out. A posse had formed up around the road entering the park for the landing.

"I've got an idea—wait there."

"Copy," I said. We set up a defense about four blocks north of the barricades. About twenty-five more minutes later Jon radioed for us to get ready to move. We packed into the transport.

"Head for the other landing point," Jon directed us.

"Why? That's too far."

"The tug is already there."

"They'll follow us."

"I'm gonna stop 'em," Jon assured me.

"Okay." We headed toward the other spot, which was about four miles away. The attacker decided not to follow us to the tug.

Once back on the island, we disembarked while Jon landed behind us on the river plane. He walked up to me and I punched his shoulder as hard as I could. "Asshole," I said to him.

"We tried to tell you," Susan told us.

CHAPTER 7

After a late lunch, Jon said, "We got four hours of day light—let's go for a ride. This is Becky, she is going to learn how to fly from Susan." Jon, Susan, Becky and I got into the plane. Susan was teaching Becky the finer points of flying while Jon and I looked out the windows. It was weird being in a plane after so long. The city had become overgrown and infested with creatures of every sort.

"There!" Jon said loudly. We looked out the window at the Butterworth house, sitting atop a hill. Overlooking the river, it was as old as hell. It had once had plenty of open lawn, but now it was planted over in various crops. During WWII, Mr. Butterworth had let the US Army use it for air defense of his factory and the island. Rumor has it that in return for his generosity, they built an elaborate underground bunker system. The best part was that it was surrounded by an eight-foot brick wall. There were about two dozen cars parked near the front door. It was the hideout for the attackers—it had to be. It was better fortified than we imagined.

"We gotta getting low on fuel," Susan said unexpectedly, so we went back to the airport. Becky's first landing was rough but she got us down. Jon and I watched the cattle grazing.

"I crave a steak," I said, making small talk.

"Next year," Jon said.

"If we last that long."

"We have to hit them before winter, really make it tough on them. Then they'll think twice about attacking us."

"How?"

"If you told me three years ago that I'd be one of 500 people left in this town, I'd call you crazy. But now I kinda envy *them*," he said nodding to the cows.

"Why?"

"They don't care that the world has gone to shit. They have food and all they do is eat, shit, fuck, and sleep. What do we have? Cold, death, hunger, hatred—and for what?! The human race deserves to be wiped clean."

"What brought this on?"

"Never mind," he said, walking back to the plane.

"Um, no," I said, grabbing his shoulder.

"I said never mind," he said, pushing my hand off.

"You can't go on a rant and not expect me to be a little worried."

"I said fucking drop it."

"Okay—consider it dropped. Do you have an idea on how to get them?"

"Yes, we take the plane out with a few cinder blocks and drop them on their fort. Then we come back and drop Molotov cocktails. Burn their fucking fort down."

"Wow. That's cruel, Dude."

"Cruel? Listen, you little fucking punk. I had to spend the fucking night out there surround by those things. Those things and the people in that house are trying to kill me. I want to kill them before they get a good shot to kill me."

"We wanted to come back."

"Oh? Right—I wouldn't let you. Fuck you. I should have."

"Sorry—I'm not a mind reader." At that, Jon stormed away.

The flight back was tense. We did a flyover to double-check the fortress, and I saw my Camaro sitting on the lawn. When we landed, Jon walked away without saying anything.

"Can we talk?" Susan said, pulling me aside.

"Sure, what's up?"

"I think he's snapped. I think everything's finally gotten to him."

"I can see your point, but he was stranded out there with you."

"Not that. He was talking about joining them." That news hit me like a cold shower.

"Which 'them'?"

"The dead ones."

"*What?*"

"He was saying maybe if he mixed his blood with that boy's, it would turn him without the pain. When I asked him if he was okay, he told me to shut the fuck up. That's when he went outside with the boy's body and proceeded to hack it up."

"Hack it up?"

"Yes, you know—take pieces and put them around the house."

"*What?*"

"I asked him what he was doing and to show some respect."

"And?"

"He just continued hacking, then waited for them."

"Zombies?"

"It's like I said—he wanted to be one."

"Do you know of anyone he talks to or anyone who knew him in the past?"

"No. He told me he was in the reserves, like you. He may not even be a local."

"Hmm. Okay, let's keep this quiet, please."

"I will."

"Thanks—and keep up the good work with Becky." We parted ways, and I headed to the mess hall to get something to eat.

"Logan—come in," my radio squawked.

"Logan here," I said.

"Can you come to the jail quick?"

"What's up?" Then it occurred to me that Jon must have gone on a rampage. "On my way," I said. I sprinted to the jail.

As I arrived, I heard Jon yelling at the prisoner named Tom. "And then I'm gonna rape your daughters!" he was yelling.

"Go get Doc—tell him to bring tranquilizers," I whispered to one of the guards. Then I said, "Jon, calm down."

"Oh—look who decided to show up. We shoulda killed them when we had the fucking chance."

"We aren't them," I said, pointing at the other two prisoners. "What makes us so different?"

"Because we don't go killing people."

"We do it daily."

"That's different—that's self-defense."

"So is killing them now. Then they can't hurt us again. What does it matter? We're gonna wipe out their hideout at the Butterworth house anyways." With that, Tom's eyes went wide almost.

"See—told you he'd give it away," Jon said, pointing at Tom.

"Okay, so you found out where they are operating out of," I said. "We aren't going to kill the prisoners."

"We?"

"We all participate in the decisions here."

"No—you and I make them all. We carry all the invalids on our backs—and for what?"

"That's not true, and you know it, Jon."

"Oh look—now Doc joining the party," Jon said.

"Calm down, Jon," Doc said.

"Don't tell me what to do, sand nigger!" The slur stopped Doc dead in his tracks.

"Jon! What the hell is wrong with you?" I shouted.

"I'm perfectly fine. I'm the realist who understand that, no matter what we do, we're all dead."

"Come on," I said.

"We're just postponing the inevitable."

"By your logic, that's what we've always done—go through life, waiting for the end."

"In those days, life was worth something. Now all I am is food for some mindless creature."

"Not if we work together. We can do this—they can't live forever."

"Oh we can?" Jon said.

"Mankind can. We were chosen, remember?"

"Oh, don't give me that crap."

"You're the one who used to say it."

"Well, things change."

"What—like you wanting to become a zombie?" I looked at Doc, who was shocked.

"Yeah—what of it? They have a simple life."

"They don't *have* a life. What's this all about?"

"You wouldn't understand."

"Try me," I said as we walked out of the room to the front of the jail.

"That girl I shot in that house? That was my sister."

"Ah, jeez—I'm sorry."

"See? You don't fucking understand. I had to find out that my sister was one of them, and then I had to kill her a split second later."

"You're right—I don't understand. But why did you hack up the zombie boy?"

"Because he turned my sister into a bloodthirsty monster who was going to kill her brother."

"How do you know he bit her?"

"See? There you go. You're so thickheaded. She stayed behind with him after she promised me she was headed to Denver. She loved him so much, but he was a piece-of-shit skateboarding druggie. He probably didn't even plan on leaving. He treated her like shit." Then Jon dropped to his knees and started to cry. Doc came from behind and hit him the tranquilizers, then we carried him to the hospital.

When we got there, a girl who couldn't have been more than sixteen was getting dressed. Doc leaned in and whispered, "That's the island's first expecting mom."

I suddenly realized there hadn't been any births in three years. I walked over to her. "Congrats."

"Oh. Thanks." she said, surprised.

"You excited?"

"I guess I am."

"You guess? That's the first baby to be conceived that I know of—hopefully the first birth too."

"I guess that's an honor. I'm just nervous about raising a baby in this world."

"Yeah, I guess. Who's the father?"

"He's gone," she said tearfully, then burst out the door.

"Garrett was the father," Doc said while untying Jon's boots.

"Oh. God*damn* it." I felt like a fool, remembering he was the boy Jon killed last night.

The next day we rested up for our final supply run. Luckily there were no attacks and the run was a success, although Jon didn't come along this trip. We had to go deeper than I wanted to, but this time we had Becky and Susan flying overhead to keep a lookout. We unloaded the supplies by floodlights—it seemed we were pushing further into the fall each year getting supplies.

A few days passed, and our "guests" was as hostile as ever. Tom, the first prisoner, was no longer rude—now he just sat there. Doc took pity on him. "We could let him go before we attack," Doc said.

"Are we going to attack?" I asked.

"If we don't, they'll keep coming."

"I hear ya." I was really hoping Jon would be back to normal, but all he did was sit in the command center or in his room. He hadn't spoken to anyone, and most everyone avoided him. He also didn't seem to be eating.

I went to see him in his room. "Doin' better?" Silence. "That good, eh? Glad to hear it. I wanted to ask, a few days ago you had a plan. What was it?" Silence still. "Wow—wild plan. I'll think about it." I got up to leave.

"Drop bombs on the house," he said softly.

"Bombs?"

"Yeah—Molotov cocktails. Set the house on fire."

"I guess that'd work."

So we had a plan, and the day after the first frost, we let Tom go and told him to get back to the house and sneak his family out. Only Becky, Susan, and Doc knew about this. They flew him out and dropped him off not too far from the house. We don't know if he and his family made it out.

Three days later, Jon and Susan took off around 11:30 p. m. We were already ashore in the troop transports with twenty armed men. The plan was to get there after the house was in flames. In the plane, Jon had four cinder blocks, three three-gallon jugs of gas, and eight cocktails. We were about forty-five minutes away when Susan made the first pass and Jon reported that the first cinder block hit the roof dead center. They made three more passes, each time hitting the roof. By the fourth pass, a large crowd formed outside the house, and those with guns were taking shots at the plane. The next pass, Jon dropped two jugs on the roof, the second one barely hitting its mark. They made another pass, and this time he followed the last one with two cocktails. As flames spread across the roof, the gunfire from the crowd intensified. Fed by the gasoline, the fire spread rapidly. Susan then lined up for an approach on their vehicles, and Jon dropped the last six in rapid succession. Four of the nine trucks and my Camaro were hit and in flames as well. The crowd saw what was happening and attempted to move the remaining trucks. They got one truck out of the way, but the other three caught fire as gas tanks around them blew up.

We showed up as Susan was lining up for the approach on the vehicles. I got on the PA speaker and said, "We can take you with us or you can die here. We tried being peaceful, but you wouldn't let us." The shots were redirected at us.

"Let them have it," I said into my radio as Susan let me know she was getting low on fuel and heading back to the airport.

One of the guys hopped out of the back and hooked a towline to the gate. Meanwhile, one of the gunners was hit, and his partner opened fire and decimated their lines. We gunned the transport and ripped the iron gate from the brick wall.

Our only injury the gunner, who was going to be okay. We headed back to base, and when we got there, we celebrated by drinking ourselves into a stupor. By the time I went to bed, I realized I'd had my first legal drink—and the next morning, I swore it would be my last.

Just before dusk that evening, Becky flew me over the ruins, and the sight was horrible. There had to be a dozen dead

children and 200 zombies. "We did that," I said to Becky. I
felt nauseous. We'd been so blinded by rage that we didn't
stop to think about the consequences. What I was able to
reconstruct was that they'd formed a human shield between
the zombies entering the hole we'd made and the kids. Their
parents probably fought bravely, but they'd been trapped between the fire and the zombies. In the end, they probably ran
out of bullets and fled. I felt so sick.

"Tell no one," I said to Becky. When we landed, I threw up.
I told Becky it was the hangover, but she felt it too. She didn't
do what I asked her, and by breakfast the next morning, I was
labeled a baby killer, murderer, etc. But the truth was, their
parents chose to wage a war on us, and we were just fighting
back. When I saw Jon, he seemed fine about the kids.

CHAPTER 8

By mid-November, work on the wall was in full swing, and people had stopped calling me names, having gradually come to accept the events, sad as they were. The wall was slowly progressing north from Sector Nine, and we decided to work north from there and work on a gate for the bridge next spring. The ground was quickly becoming rock hard, and in my gut I knew this was going to be a bad winter.

Jon was still a shadow of himself, so everything was left up to me. I went to the command center to see how things were going, and when I got there, President Bishop was in the middle of a speech. The operator pointed at a tape recorder, so I went outside to take a leak. By the time I got back inside, the speech was over and I listened to the tape.

"Good day, my fellow Americans. I bear good and bad news—and I'll start with the bad. We're losing the war on all four fronts. The undead soldiers are relentless. We're running out of ammunition on all fronts. The quarantine of the Pacific Northwest is rapidly losing ground as former Seattle citizens that survived the napalm attack have finally reached our lines. Our boys are hanging tough. The Royal Canadian Army is backed clear up to the Yukon. Sadly, Her Majesty's envoy arrived on Canadian shores swarming with dead British. Our forces in the north are working with Canadian troops to beat them back. Winter freezes the zombies, and they thaw out in the spring and resume their unholy mission. The Mexican Army has collapsed—rioting among troops led to their demise. They protested their government's actions and revolted. The zombies quickly disposed of the Mexicans, and our boys in the South and Southwest have retreated to a new defensive perimeter. As of now, plans to reclaim Southern California have been put on hold. Our forces in the East have stopped their advance just short of the Iowa border. Sadly, with the onset of a harsh Midwest winter, I've ordered their retreat so they can rearm and regroup for the spring campaign. As most of you know from my previous speeches, General Scudheigh is recruiting troops. Do not fall for his tricks. He went rogue and started killing civilians. His troops were quickly dispatched by our special forces when we discovered he was killed by one of his slaves. There are no authorized safe havens beyond the eastern lines.

Now the good news. We've established a path to the sea from the tip of Oregon to the middle of California, and the super-fort of Denver is still strong. The walls are two-foot-thick concrete. The downside is, the land we use for food production is less than ideal and less protected. We have barely enough food to feed ourselves, although next year will be different. But it is with a heavy heart that as of today, November 6, the US government, which has been a shining example of democracy throughout the world, will cease to exist. In order to ensure the survival of our species, we must be less of a democracy and more like a military force. I will still be in charge of the provisional government from the island of Maui. But General Rick West will take over from here. In a few minutes I will turn it over to him, but as soon as the crisis is over, democracy will be restored. That is all. God bless the United States of America." I was shocked by what I'd heard so far—they were giving up on us, and mankind.

General West sounded like your average general—a strong military type. "Before I begin, it's not easy being the man who suspended democracy, but in order for our families to survive, sacrifices must be made. I've served in Bosnia, Iraq, and Afghanistan. I was in Berlin when the wall came down, so I do know a few things about fighting a war. That being said, let me explain what's happening outside the US. What we know is, Britain and the rest of the Western Europe have fortified the Iberian Peninsula and stopped the advancement of the large zombie plague. Russia, Eastern Europe, the Med, Africa, most of China, a large portion of Japan have been overrun. Ironically, the South and North Koreans have worked to reinforce the 38thparallel. Italy has been able to stop the tide at the town of Castrovillari. The Greek Islands,

Cyrus, and Sicily are mostly safe. The Pacific islands are hit or miss—unconfirmed reports state that all islands are overrun. Australia has been ninety-five percent infected. Obviously, Antarctica is safe, but attempts to reach our expeditions there have failed. We believe they ran out of supplies and perished. The same can be said of our men in the International Space Station. The disease was temporarily stopped by the Panama Canal, but quickly spread through South America as refugees arrived. The once-proud British and American navies have turned to looting. Few ships are loyal to the US or UK because they feel we turned our backs on them. Luckily, most crews weren't onboard before the outbreak, or the ship suffered an outbreak. Most ships that went rogue have been destroyed. Now that everyone is up to speed, we cannot to continue to fight a four-front war and expect to win. That is why I've ordered our eastern divisions back to the original line of defense, using the Rockies as a defensive barrier. We know the zombies are struggling with the winters and the mountains in the East. The zombies can't survive in the extreme cold. We'll send extra divisions to clear out the Pacific Northwest. Once that's safe, we'll leave a small contingent to defend the border area. Next we'll clear out the So Cal region, and then sweep into Mexico, because the desert is so vast, we won't be able to maintain a line. Therefore the remainder of our gunships and drones and bombers will patrol the southern skies, either attacking or keeping tabs on the zombies. We still maintain strike teams along the southern border, and once those tasks are accomplished in partnership with the other North American countries, we'll begin a slow march across the continent. We expect to reach Iowa by next fall, a little less than a year from now. Thank you and God bless." I was speechless when Jon said, "Yep—figures."

"We have two years to go—we can easily make that," I said to everyone in the room. I got onto the PA and told everyone the gist of what we'd just heard. Few people were surprised.

While work on the wall continued, I helped build wind-mills. We put them rooftops for maximum efficiency, and each typically provided enough power for that home—better than nothing. I found two farmers with cows, and they started clearing a pasture around the boulder. Next to it would be a pig farm, and next to that a hen house. Pigs would be hard to find, but cattle and chicken were plentiful at the airport. Two of the prisoners, earned their release by helping us build those windmills. That's when I first really met Jade. He was working on the windmill, I had never seen him around be-fore, but he was such a big man it was hard to not notice him.

With three projects going, winter flew by. One day in Jan-uary, one of the guards noticed some people on the bridge. They had a giant sign that said "Help!" By this time, the temperature was hovering around ten in the day and thirty below at night. I went up with Jade and the two former pris-oners who'd joined our cause after learning their compadres' fate, They'd turned out to have useful skills—one had been an electrician for the power company and was showing us how to wire in the windmills. Jade was the second-shift com-mander who'd stepped up as Jon withdrew.

We rowed to the bridge and found them ducked behind a car. "Don't kill us," a voice said. My comrades had their guns out. I chuckled. Was it a trap? We crouched behind two cars. "Show yourselves! " I yelled. Seven figures slowly rose from behind the car. I stood up to see them—seven women all looking close to thirty, wrapped in blankets and parkas covered in blood.

"We have no weapons," one of the women said.

"I'd like to believe that," I said.

"Logan? Is that you?" said the woman.

"Yes?" I said hesitantly.

"It's me—Michelle . . . from high school?" Michelle was my first real girlfriend, back in the ninth grade. We went our separate ways when she decided I was holding her back. From what—a douche bag who was a junior and on the baseball team? She'd broken my heart then, but I was over her by now. Besides, I had a zombie apocalypse on my hands.

"Holy crap. How're you?" I asked.

She laughed lightly. "Never been better."

"Who are your friends?" I realized they were younger than they looked. Michelle certainly was.

"This is Kara, and Shawna, my older sister, Zoey, Nikki, Natasha, and Alaina." Each girl said hi, except Kara.

"We need six female inspectors up here," I radioed.

"Inspectors?" said Michelle.

"Yeah—to make sure you weren't bitten," Jade said.

"I don't want to make you uncomfortable by having a guy inspect you," I said.

"You can inspect me anytime," Michelle said with a smile.

"Maybe later," I said. Michelle and another of the girls stayed with me on the bridge while the overloaded rowboat worked against the current. Then I thought to myself, *a rope.* That's would make it easier. I pulled out a little notebook and wrote down "rope" and the reason.

"What's that?" Michelle said, pointing at the notebook.

"Pocket Brain—supplies we need, things to get, etc."

"That's better than the Logan I used to know."

"Um, thanks? I don't think I've changed that much." The boat came back and we rowed back to the island. The other guys and I knew we hadn't been bitten and convinced to look away. After twenty minutes, the girls reemerged with fresh clothes. I asked them if they had any special skills. Alaina said she'd been studying to be a doctor. Nikki and Natasha, brown-haired, brown-eyed twins had been in the 4-H Club in high school. Shawna had been a mechanical engineer with a small construction firm. We hit it lucky with these girls.

We took a tour of the island. The golf carts were useless in the snow, but we had sleds we could pull with snowmobiles and a few four-wheelers. Shawna was feeling ill, so we ended the tour at the hospital and Doc looked over the girls. He said they were in surprisingly good health, except for Shawna. He sent her to the sick house, which was some distance from the other homes. Since medicine was so limited, it was best to isolate those who were ill. It made Doc's job easier.

Life was back to normal the next week. The sixth day after the girls arrived, Michelle came to visit me in my office. I had taken over the base CO's office, since I was effectively in charge. She closed the door behind her. "What happened to us?" she asked.

"A zombie outbreak, or hadn't you heard?"

"No—*us*."

"If memory serves, you dumped me for Dan because he had a car."

"Did I? I never meant to hurt you."

"It was the ninth grade. I've had plenty of time to get over it."

"Yeah. You're doing a bang-up job."

"Thanks. Whatever happened with you and Dave?"

"Ha! That lasted all of a month. He just wanted in my pants. I thought he really loved me, but after I gave him my special flower, he was gone—just like that."

"Ouch—his loss."

"Yeah, sure. I saw him not too long ago."

"Oh? How is he?"

"Dead."

"Oh, how nice."

"No—you killed him."

I froze. "What do you mean?" I said.

"We know it was your people that attacked us."

"Then why did you ask for our help?"

"Because it was better than the other option. We were gonna starve out there." Tears started forming in her big brown eyes.

"I'm sorry, but your people attacked us first."

"I know, but you basically turned your back on us."

"You shot at us when we offered assistance," I said, rage building up inside me.

"*I* did no such thing! Most of us were in the bunker. That's where he kept us!"

"Kept you?"

"Mooney. He and his boys raped us daily, sometimes more often. More after someone pissed him off."

"Are you talking about me?" I asked, feeling a pang of guilt.

"Oh, the island in general, I guess." She paused. "He was so cruel to us."

"I'm sorry," I said, meaning it.

"I know you are, but you killed at least fifty kids. How do you sleep? Or don't you care?"

"I have 248 people to worry about. It was this basic—us or them. I didn't want to do it, and had I known how many deaths I'd cause, I would've thought harder about it. But you guys got caught in the crossfire. I'm truly sorry for your losses, but I stand by my actions."

"I didn't come here for reasoning, or an apology."

"Why did you then?"

"To thank you. You coulda just left us to die. We were ambushed several times. Poor Shawna had to kill our cousin with her bare hands, just two nights ago. Now she has the flu, three years and she's survived that, but now?"

"She'll be fine. Doc's seen a lot worse."

"I hope."

"You're welcome though."

"Who woulda thunk you'd be my savior all along," she said, smiling. We spent the next few hours talking about our lives both before and after the outbreak. It was nearing eleven p. m., and I yawned and offered to walk her home.

"Home?"

"Yeah. Aren't you staying on the island?"

"If you'll let us."

"Well, I'll have to think about that. You did try to kill me."

"Did not—*stop!*"

"All right. I'm sure we can find something for you to do."

"Ha—thanks." We started walking toward the housing complex. I refused a ride and trudged in the snow with

Michelle. After a cold thirty-minute hike, we made it to where she was staying.

"Well, take care, Kiddo."

"That's it?" she said curiously.

"You're welcome?"

"Thanks?"

"For walking you home?"

"God. You are still thick-headed."

"Okay. Good night?"

"Night," she said frostily, and went inside. After walking about a block, I realized what had just transpired. Idiot. I could have had a shot with her. I hadn't thought about sex in years. Funny how life throws you curve balls. The next morning, a woman named Karen asked me if they were really going to stay.

"Yes, why not?"

"Why? They tried to kill us."

"They were sex slaves, not soldiers," I said.

"Oh well that makes it better," she said, then walked away. Word spread quickly, thanks to Becky and Karen, who were apparently the island gossip queens. Thank God, that was the case because no one else bothered me about why they were staying. Everyone was adapting to island life—well everyone but Jon. He slept in the jailhouse locked in the cell, with a shotgun cradled in his arms. He was falling apart.

Two days later I ran into Michelle at lunch. "Fancy meeting you here," she said.

"Turns out this is the only place with food."

"Sarcasm—nice."

"Yeah. So tonight we're going to watch *Dawn of the Dead*. Interested?"

"A zombie movie? Seriously?"

"We view it as a comedy," I said.

"Sure," she said hesitantly.

"Meet you at your house?"

"I'll be ready at 5:30."

"You gonna get all dolled up?"

"Maybe not now."

"Aww, I'm sorry."

I showed up to her house at five, and surprisingly she was ready to go. "Wow—you look amazing," I said.

"More sarcasm. You know how to sweep a girl off her feet."

"I was serious."

"Oh—well thanks then." We walked through the snow to the gym. We sat on folding chairs and watched it was weird in that moment it actually felt like normal again. The movie ended and we got some apple juice. Then we walked out into a brewing snowstorm.

"My house is just over there, it's only a five-minute walk. You can spend the night."

"What are you suggesting, Mister?"

"Hey—not that. I can sleep elsewhere. I share a room with other people."

"Oh. Well sure, I guess." We walked into the house as the snow started falling more heavily.

"Hold on a sec." I went into the kitchen and radioed, "Code White." Two minutes later, an announcement went out over the PA for all non-essential personnel return to their homes, heavy snow expected.

"Look at you," she said as she unbuttoned her jacket.

"Perks of the job." I pulled out two chairs and we sat at the table, listening to the wind howl and talking about our pasts. When I looked at the clock on the wall, it read 4 a. m.

"I'm going to go to bed. Coming?" she asked, standing up.

"I gotta brush my teeth."

"Cute."

"Seriously, I do." And after finishing up, I crept into my room, which I shared with three others. I looked at my bed and there she lay. "It's cold. Get in here—you'll freeze on the floor." I didn't hesitate—I put my radio and pistol on the nightstand lay down facing away from her.

"Does my breath smell that bad?" she said. I rolled over and looked in her beautiful doe eyes. Without hesitation, I leaned in and kissed her. She returned my kiss, then pulled away. "Goodnight, Logan."

"Goodnight, Michelle." I stared at her beauty awhile before I fell drifted off.

CHAPTER 9

But my sleep was interrupted by a banging on my bedroom door. It was Doc, and he was covered in blood. "What happened?"

"I had to kill them all."

"*What?* Who?" Out of breath, he explained that at 6 a. m., like always, he went to the alternate hospital, basically a house that was fitted with extra beds to keep up with the growing number of sick, to check on everyone and found the front door wide open. There were footprints in the snow—and blood. He didn't carry a radio, so he ran into the house and used a steak knife to stab all of new zombies in the head before they could turn. He saw three were missing.

I grabbed my radio and called a Code Red. Almost instantaneously the PA came alive. "This is a Code Red. Repeat—this is a Code Red." It was quickly followed by the siren. "This is not a drill. Report to your stations. This is not a drill."

I turned around. Michelle had my gun leveled at Doc. "It wasn't enough to kill the people I used to live with? Now you killed my sister?"

"Stop," I said.

"Why?"

"Because we don't know if she was bitten—she could have escaped. She wasn't that sick."

"She slipped into a coma yesterday morning," Michelle said.

"What? A virulent flu?" I asked.

"I'm not sure she had the flu," Doc said. We looked at him. "She wasn't responding to the drugs we gave her."

"Let's go. You two go to the gym." She tried to hand me the gun. "Keep it—you may need it," I said. I kissed her forehead and said it'd be all right. I sprinted to the command center to direct the forces. "Where is everyone?" I asked when I got there. Only about ten had arrived before me.

"The snow's too deep—people are trapped in their houses. It's close to three feet deep when you get off the main roads," the shift commander, my familiar friend Ryan Rumler, said.

"Shit." I grabbed the PA mic and took a deep breath. "Code Red, Code Red. Return to your homes and lock the doors. If you are closer to the gym and can make it, then do so. But if you are closer to a house, then go there. Put a sign in the front window telling us how many people are in the house. We'll distribute food and other supplies till the storm clears." When I realized everyone was staring at me, I said, "What—you have any better ideas?" They didn't have any. There were twelve of us there now. I sent six on snowmobiles and sleds to the gym, and there they divided up—four on the roof and two at the door. The other five took off to round up the patrolling guards and stragglers. "Take them to the gym. Once you have a count, come back with guards and get more snowmobiles. Get all the raiders you can muster up here." Once everyone had their marching orders, they took off. I locked the door behind them.

"No movement at the water plant," a woman's voice said.

"How many do you have there?"

"Six."

"Okay. Stay in a warm place. Lock the doors and windows."

"Already done."

"If you see—"

"I'll tell you, but the snow's getting worse," she said, cutting me off.

"I know."

The minutes ticked by slowly until the radio came to life. "We're there," said one of the guards I'd sent to the gym. "We count Doc and seven others, locking the doors."

"Good luck."

"I count seven possible stragglers. They're not bitten—they're inside," the guard said.

"By my count, there should be 256 people," I said.

"Did you count the girls and the two deaths, yesterday?" Doc said.

"I think the girls count, but the roster doesn't show any deaths," Ryan said.

"They died in the hospital, shortly after midnight," Alaina said, who had been assisting Doc with the patients.

"Thanks, Hospital. Are you locked in?"

"No sign of them here—our doors are locked. We moved everyone into the back three rooms and moved a bed against the back and side doors," she replied.

"What's your count?" I asked.

"Twelve, including myself," she said. I wrote the numbers on a piece of paper to keep track.

"Doc, how many people were in the house?"

"He says around twenty—he can't remember exactly," Brandon, the guard from the gym, answered.

"How many people did he kill?"

"He's not positive, but fifteen or sixteen."

"Everyone listen up—we've got six to eight zombies out there."

"Or alive," Alaina said.

"Either way, we've got to find them before it gets worse out there."

"We've got all the patrollers—we're headed back to base," one of the guys said. Just then I jumped when I heard banging on the front door. I picked up my gun and went to the door. It was a woman I'd seen around but couldn't remember her name. She had blood all over her parka.

"I can't let you in," I said into the intercom. She pleaded with me and started begging for help, but stopped midsentence when two slow-moving creatures appeared out the shadows behind her. She punched the first, a young boy dressed in sweat pants, in the head. He staggered a bit before pressing forward regretting what was about to happen I pulled the gun from my holster, the woman looked back at me and pleaded with me to do it. I took aim and fired a shot at her head. Thunk. She was still standing, unbeknownst to me the glass was bullet proof and had stopped the bullet. I wasn't going to risk my life to stop the carnage, so I went back into the control room. I could hear her scream as the two hungry creatures devoured her.

"We got two at the gym," Brandon said. The creatures were finishing up the woman when the first of the five snow-mobiles returned. They shot all three of them in the head and I let them in.

"We got to figure out a way out of this," Jade said, removing his snow cap.

"We can't put them all in the gym. What if one was bitten? We don't have time to inspect them all," I said to them.

"Three groups—mess hall, gym, and the warehouse would be the best way to divide everyone," Jade said.

"I'd rather not use the warehouse—it's too open. Plus, what if one was bitten in there? Then we'd have no food. But I do like your plan. I think we should use the mess hall, gym, and the office building across the street from the gym."

"Office building?" Jade said.

"Yeah. We don't use it, and there's a fallout shelter in the basement." At that point, we had thirty people in the command center. I sent Jade and Simon to the water tower to be lookouts, since that was the highest point on the island. I sent another three to the gym as reinforcements. The plan was to take a hundred to the gym, a hundred to the mess hall, and the remainder to the fallout shelter. Seventeen guards would secure the mess hall while ten would form a convoy and start routing people to the gym. I stayed in the warmth of the command center, eating a Snickers bar. The base had a minimal security camera system, but we kept it turned off to save power. I turned it on and slowly a few grainy images started appearing on the monitors.

"I see something," Simpson, from the roof, said. Someone came from the gym to get the slow moving person, and as the guard from the gym approached the snow-covered figure, he smelled blood. The guard, a sixteen year old boy, froze, his blood as cold as the snow he was standing in. I watched from a distance as the zombie turned toward the young guard, who snapped to his senses and stumbled back. He fired his pistol six times, all body shots, and the zombie fell over. The kid quickly scrambled to his feet and ran all the way back to the gym. While this was transpiring, the first snowmobiles made it to the houses, and people were told to bring warm clothes. The convoy took off for the gym, with about twenty-five people on sleds in tow. The snowmobiles were unarmed, and I told them to stop for nothing. It would take fifteen minutes to get back to the gym. Five guards formed up in the center of the road. The visibility was staring to get better.

At the mess hall, the party leader reported in. "First floor secured, moving up."

"Copy," I said. The mess hall had two other, less spacious floors, which were ready to receive guests. Six guys stayed behind to secure it while the remaining eleven went to the fallout shelter. It wasn't connected to the office building, as we thought, but accessed by a staircase just outside. That would make it easier to defend. On the other side was a fire escape that led to the roof.

"Ewww. It's clear, but I say we use it as a last resort. It smells horrible, it's damp, and there are rats down here," a voice said over the radio.

"Understand," I said. "Leave three guys there, one on the roof and two inside. Alternate to stay warm or stay out of the smell. The remaining eight should start picking up people. Take as many snowmobiles as you can." Within two hours, the gym was full and the mess hall was getting people from the hospital. Then a group of guards who had been trans-porting people stayed to help defend the mess hall. The sun was starting to break through the clouds, visibility was improving.

"Has anyone seen Jon?" Jade said, breaking the silence.

"Now that you mention it, no," I said. "When you get a chance, swing by the jail."

"We got one more load, and I think that's it," said the snowmobile driver.

"All stations report your numbers," I said.

"Gym—116, including guards."

"Mess hall—seventy-seven, including guards."

"Fallout shelter, three."

"Water station still six."

"That's 202?" I asked.

"Well, 205 including base," Jade said.

"Okay, so that's forty-eight unaccounted for," I said. That was too many to just wait it out." Gym, give me thirty able-bodied people—preferably men we use for offensive missions. Once they finish loading up the mess hall, I'll have the guards pick them up and come here to arm up."

"I think you're gonna have to redirect those forces," Jade said nervously.

"We need to sweep the island."

"Well, look—there," pointing to the ice, "the ice is almost hard enough for those monsters to cross."

"What?"

"The ice between Illinois and the island is probably about a foot shy of forming an ice bridge."

"Will the troop transports work in the snow?"

"Not sure."

"Jade, can you hold them off?"

"We don't have enough ammo for that. They're having a hard enough time with the ice as it is. It's not completely formed up, but it may be in other areas."

"It'll be dark soon, and we have no way of defending on two fronts attacks if that ice freezes we are boned. Gym, get as many people as you can to the roof." I grabbed the mic and said, "Quick status update: there are forty-eight people unaccounted for. There are at least twenty confirmed deaths. If you aren't at the gym, mess hall, or water department, get to the nearest shelter and lock yourself in. Figure out a way to get our attention here. The main buildings have fire alarms, and my panel will tell me where you are. I'll send a snowmobile as soon as I can. Our other problem is that the ice on the Illinois side is almost thick enough for them to walk on.

We've never had that problem before. For now we're going to deal with the outside threat. Stay in the mess hall and gym. Food will be brought when it can." I put down the mic.

The guys from the gym arrived a few minutes after I was finished. "Here's what we're going to do," I told them." I'll take twenty with me to the housing complex. We'll do a sweep and try to get a count of the dead and find any stragglers. Ten of you get ten more guys and to get about five small cans of gas. Throw gas on the ice and light it. That should melt it. I'll have the guys from the fallout shelter try to get the troop transport there. If it can make it in the snow, use the big guns. If it's not there by sundown, fall back to base" Several shots rang out.

"Simon's trying his best, but there's a solid patch by the Moline Bridge," Jade informed us.

"Get some dry wood too," I said, finishing up. We went our separate ways. I locked the scared teenager alone in the control room. The sun reflecting off the snow made it hard to see. Sporadic shots continue to ring out from the water tower. Within fifteen minutes, we were to the first row of houses. "Hello, is anyone out there?" No response. Not wanting to risk any casualties, we split into two teams of ten. Tristan, the last remaining original shift commander, was put in charge of the other group. We took the right side and they took the left. Both houses were empty, but we tore them apart, just to be safe. They'd already moved onto the second house when shots rang out.

"I found five semi-dead victims," Tristan said. We were down to forty-three missing people. Meanwhile, as Jade was getting Simon more ammo, Simon got an unexpected visitor just below him. He shot it twice in the face.

"One down inside the fence. I think he was an island resident. But I think the ice is starting to give out by the bridge," Simon reported.

"We'll still melt it," the group leader said. About a dozen shots rang out." Three down by the warehouse." It was now

mid-afternoon. By the time I got to the other side of the island, Simon was still shooting away, but he'd gotten down
from the water tower and was closer to the mainland in one
of the old outpost. There he had a clean shot at the bridge
and the ice.

"It's starting to give way, but they're still coming," he said,
reading my mind. The other group showed up right before I
did and was propping a ladder against the wall. A few guys
were up on the wall throwing old soup cans full of gas onto
the ice. A man named James climbed up the ladder took aim
at the one of the zombies with a crossbow and hit him in the
chest with a flaming arrow. This caused the zombie to stumble into the icy water. That's when that group of guys got a
crazy idea. Three of them volunteered to jump the wall, each
carrying two containers of gas. Then, as quickly as the fresh
snow allowed, they made their way to the bridge. From there
they dumped the gas on a zombie wearing medical scrubs.
Then James aimed for its head with the flaming arrow and
got it in the left eye. The zombie burst into flames, and several other zombies nearby also caught on fire. Significantly,
the ice started to give way under the weight of the burning
zombies, and within moments they burned right through the
ice. For the time being, their only means of crossing had been
eliminated. The men then retraced their steps under Simon's
watchful eyes and climbed back over the wall. Their vehicles
barely had any traction in the soft snow—one transport was
already stuck after about a hundred feet—so they hiked over
to the gym to warm up.

The sun was quickly ducking behind clouds again. I asked
the guys if they'd be brave enough to jump the wall again.
They said they would, and this time they'd take floodlights
and set them in the snow aimed at the mainland. For the time
being this would be our first line of defense. Jade and Simon
moved back up to the tower. Jade now carried two sleeping bags and some road flares in case of an emergency. Before the sun went down, the guys jumped the wall and ran

extension cords for the floods, which lit up the night and cast ghostly shadows off the zombies.

"Barbed wire," I said to myself, jotting it down in my notebook.

That night, ten guys stayed in the security center, and the other ten delivered a six-day supply of food to the gym. We hoped it wouldn't take that long, but it was better safe than sorry. Jade and Simon took turns watching and counting the number of zombies that fell into the river. They had no balance or traction, and several would go in at once. Simon was shooting at them. Nineteen guys and I packed up into the corner house we'd already cleared. We made sure all the doors were locked. We put the five dead bodies in the center of the road and burned them. At about 4:30 in the morning, I woke everyone up. We had no food, and we still had to clear out ten more rows of houses. Thank God, for city planners and making the clearing out easier. It was dead silent outside, and sunrise was a long way off. By seven, a fringe of sun began to show, and twenty guys went to the wall. I sent fifteen to get food and told them to meet us at the third row. I asked Jade, "How'd you sleep?"

"Cold as fuck up here. My balls are frozen together," he said, probably expecting me to remind him I slept in a warm house. I sent two guys from the gym to replace them so they could warm up. Once the additional fifteen more got there, we had cold spaghetti and then broke into four teams of eight. The three remaining guys watched the road. It was that eerie quiet. It took us until eleven to finish the third row, and then we moved onto the fourth. Since all the houses had the same basic floor plan, we'd gotten pretty efficient at clearing them. The four throw was done by two, and the fifth by five p. m. It was already dark, and we were all tired. Jade and Simon returned to their posts, and we again we crashed into a corner house. The four remaining rows would go quicker because most were empty and should have been locked.

Around 2 a.m, a guard on the mess hall roof spotted movement coming down the main road. He shouted, but the figure kept coming. In deep snow, zombies and humans moved alike. When the figure ignored a second warning, he shot it, hitting it in the calf. It went down.

CHAPTER 10

"You're supposed to aim for the head, fucking retard," the figure yelled. It was Jon. I wasn't there, but the guard filled me in. Jon had been looking for survivors on a snowmobile when he flipped. Two guys from the mess hall went down to get him. He sent them back, but they left him a radio. On his way back, he'd come across a pack zombies. He was sure he'd killed all but two.

"Are you okay?" I asked Jon, over the radio circuit, as I got dressed and headed downstairs from the house I had been spending the night in.

"Well, let's see: I'm freezing, I've been shot—and, more importantly, I was bitten. Son of a bitch caught me while I was pissing. Luckily I moved, or he would have got me in a bad spot."

"You know, we almost—"

"I know—that's why I came into town. I tried to do myself in, but needless to say I couldn't."

"We can bring you in and let you die warm," I offered.

"Nah—I think the cold is slowing down the transformation, but thanks. I'm sorry."

"For what?" I asked, even though I knew what he was sorry for.

"For becoming a selfish prick."

"Its all good. I'd feel the same if I shot my sister, even in self-defense."

"Yeah. I hope you don't have to."

"Thanks, but I have that feeling someone else already has."

"Never know. The Lord works in mysterious ways."

"Found God again?"

"Never lost Him. I lost my faith in mankind. We did this, and God is just wiping the wretched from the earth—present company included."

"You think so?" I jumped onto a snowmobile. I wasn't about to let my best friend die alone in the cold.

"I do. Why else would he have let me suffer with all this survivor's guilt? I close my eyes and I'm tortured by the faces of people I never met, but set into motion their demise. I killed, what—a hundred women and children because of what happened to us? I was enraged at my sister, her loser boyfriend, you, everything, and I killed them. I'm not worthy to be alive."

"Me?" I said." It was self-defense. You had no way of knowing zombies would trap them."

"We could have just burned down the house, and you were being all squeamish about torture and killing the captives. They tried to kill us. Luckily Simon stopped them."

"You're right on both counts."

"No reaction?" he said.

"I admitted I was skittish and we shouldn't have gone to such extremes. Things would be different."

"Yeah—I wouldn't be dying."

"I guess. But they'd eventually get you. They're pretty determined."

"I think I'd rather die by gunfire."

"Yeah—that definitely has its upside," I acknowledged.

"Shit!"

"What?"

"I think they followed me," Jon said.

"Can they do that?"

"I see some coming toward me."

"How far?"

"Maybe a block away."

"I'm almost there," I said, revving the engine of the snowmobile.

"Well, hurry—I've got just one lucky shot left." I gunned the worn-out snowmobile, and within minutes my headlamp hit his snow covered body. I coasted to a stop and swathe transformation was in effect. His skin was paler, his eyes were bloodshot, and sinking in.

"Aren't you a sight for sore eyes," he said.

"Where are they?" I asked. He nodded toward the road, and I hopped onto the snowmobile. I saw them—there were five—and I pulled within ten feet and fired five shots. They all went down. I approached them and recognized all five. One was a guy I'd seen barely two days ago—he'd sat in front of me at the movie with Michelle. I suddenly remembered all about them." The five new girls, whose got them?" I whispered into my radio.

"I got four at the gym," Brandon said.

"There's one here at the mess hall, "another guard said from the mess hall.

"Gym, quietly take one guy with you and take those girls and the other one to the jail."

"Uh, why?"

"I'll explain when I get there." Deep down I knew they were innocent, but the timing was too coincidental. I inched the snowmobile back to Jon. There was a lake of frozen blood under him.

"I haven't got much time, but thanks for coming," he said looking up at me.

"You'd do the same for me."

"Not so sure of that. I would have shot you years ago, if I didn't need you."

"What?" His comment sent a chill down my spine.

"Sure—everyone needs you. They needed the compassionate one when Lewis was in charge. You knew what needed to be done and did it. I was confident in the fact that I never had to ask or volunteer—I knew you'd do it. That's why you've always been in charge. I was envious at first. I wanted you to be left out there that first night. But if you had been, I doubt we'd have survived this long. You knew what we needed and didn't need. I wanted the leadership role, but you were such a natural at it. They needed you as much as I did. I had no problems sending kids to meet their maker, but you fought alongside 'em."

He coughed up blood as I stood there numbed by the cold, and by the callous words from a man I'd trusted with my

life." Surprised?" he said, smiling, blood still caked on his
teeth. I was still too shocked to say anything to him, so I
just nodded. I wasn't angry—I was livid. I raised up my pistol and he started to cry. Tears were flowing down his face,
freezing on his pale skin. "I'm sorry—I wouldn't kill you. I
was just jealous. I don't wanna die." He started to cough up
more blood." I lied—I don't hate you. Please, don't kill me.
Let me die . . . I don't wanna die. I can't be one of them—I
don't want that curse."

I was torn. I knew he was trying to make me mad enough
to shoot him, but he was my friend." You really got twelve?"
I said as I lowered my pistol.

"Yeah."

He didn't have a weapon." With what?"

"My rifle. It got too heavy, so I hid it in some bushes. If
only I could drive those damn things, I wouldn't have flipped
and I wouldn't have dislocated my shoulder again. That's
how those fuckers got me. They got me while I was down,"
he said, wiping the last of his frozen tears.

"Can I see the wound?" He slid up his right coat sleeve.
Sure enough—mingled with the blood and torn fabric was a
human bite mark, the skin around it was oozing pus and full
of blisters.

"Hurts like hell," he said.

"I bet."

"You know, I didn't want you dead—I just wanted you to
not feel guilty about what you gotta do."

"I know, but there's nothing I can do about this situation.
I'll feel guilty regardless. You're a good man."

"Thanks, but I *was* a good man."

"Ha sure." He reached into his overcoat pocket and handed
me a pristine silver-plated Colt revolver with a pearl handle.
I recognized it.

"We got it at that trucking company. I never took the bullet
out. I had a feeling it was meant for me. Scary, huh?"

"No—fate." I looked in the cylinder, and sure enough—a
single bullet.

"Sorry I didn't save you a shot," he said.

"Thanks. I wouldn't want to carry around the gun that I knew was meant for me."

"Well, I am a freak. I don't want to rush you, but I'm starting to get sleepy."

"Close your eyes, old friend."

"Try not to miss me." He closed his eyes, and I sat there staring at him blankly. By now the wind had died down and the sun was starting to come up. I knew people at the gym and mess hall were watching through binoculars. Slowly his breath became more shallow as the end neared. I sat there and watched as his final breath left his body. I heard a bird call overhead. I looked down at my friend's body, took a deep breath, and stood up. The zombie Jon awoke, and before it could let out a sorrowful moan, I shot my friend in the center of his forehead. The body landed with a thud. I put the gun back into this steely cold hands, then rode over to the jail with tears streaming down my face.

The sun up by the time I got to the jail." Start on the sixth row," I said into the radio, "same as before. I'll be there when I can."

"Copy that," Tristan said.

"Everyone—my radio will be off. Jade is in charge." Before anyone could protest, I turned it off and put it on the seat of the snowmobile. Then I turned to the two outside guards." Listen—I know they're innocent. Keep them isolated until we're safe and clear of zombies. People are going to think they did this, but they lost one just like us. I don't want a blood bath because people are angry. Understood? I'm gonna ask you both, do you believe they're innocent?" They both nodded." Good. Keep an eye out. They couldn't go anywhere, but if the girls stayed, their lives were in danger." I went into the jailhouse.

"Why are we here?" Nikki said.

"Because if we stay at the gym, they'd kill us," Michelle said.

"What?" Alaina said, looking at Michelle, then at me.

"Because of the timing, and because my sis was in the house it started in," Michelle explained.

"You don't think she was bitten," Natasha asked me.

"She wasn't when she got here, but I know she's gone now," Michelle said.

"I'm so sorry," Alaina said, then to me she said, "Is that why we're here? You think we did it?"

"They tried to kill us before—why not finish the job?" Nikki said, sitting down next to Michelle.

"That's not why you're here," I finally said. "I believe you're innocent. But the other people have nothing to do but imagine the worst."

"What about the ones in the mess hall who are sick? Doc and the nurses are in the gym," Alaina said. I went outside and grabbed the radio.

"Jade, get a nurse over to the mess hall to take care of the remaining sick," I said into the radio.

"Doc is already on his way over," Jade said. He was great at details. I went back inside.

"Problem solved. I need you guys to stay here, in case things get out of hand. The jail is made of reinforced cinder blocks and steel. You'll be fine," I said to the girls. They thanked me as I left.

"Radio's on—what did I miss?" I asked.

"Nothing here. The ice is melting and they just said they're finishing up the sixth row of houses, "Jade said, as he was becoming more comfortable with his leadership role.

"Now we have a problem," Tristan's voice said very nervously.

"What?", I said.

"We've got two dead here, but there's way too much blood for just two. They look like they were killed before they turned," Tristan said.

"What house number was it?" I said as I approached the housing area.

"Number 644."

"Gym, get the people from that address outside," I directed as I turned around and headed back toward the gym. I got there in ten minutes and waited. Nothing, I went to the door and knocked. No answer. "Gym, you want to let me in?" The door opened quickly.

"Get in here," a young boy said, scared "They're rioting."

"What?" I said, "What happened?"

"I asked if anyone knew who was in number 644, and everyone in the gym directed me to an old couple, a family of four and a family of six. When I approached them, they refused to come with me and the folks around us got hostile and started throwing things. We bolted and left," the head guard said.

"Okay—let me try this." I went up the back stairs into the old bleachers and, using a bullhorn I found in the lobby, said, "Let me have your attention. We're trying to protect you. We just want the families of house 644. There was two dead zombies in that home and we just want to be safe." The crowd grew more rowdy, and someone hit me with a can of soup. I pulled out my pistol and fired a shot into the air, and the room became silent. "I was trying to be calm about this, but today isn't the day to piss me off. I just had to kill Jon Greene after he became a zombie. So if you think adding more people to my list will bother me, think again. The most important thing is to check that none of the people in the house were bitten. I applaud your efforts for killing two zombies, but we have to work together. I'm sorry for the commotion, but time is of the essence. If you lived in that house or were in that house, please come up to the stage." Reluctantly the twelve people walked up to the bleachers, and I climbed down and took them to a locker room. "Who wants to tell me what happened?"

"We heard sirens and started to get dressed," the father of the four kids said, "When I went outside, three of those things were on top of me. The two dead guys save my life—they grabbed me. One was pulled back out into the snow. The second grabbed for his buddy and was bitten. They fought them off, and the first one limped into the bathroom. That's probably the blood you saw. They gave us a revolver. I knew we had to do it, so I shot them before they changed."

"Okay, that's all good, but why did you stonewall us?" I said, sitting on the bench.

"Because of the third guy who was bitten," he responded.

"What third guy? I thought you said two guys pulled you out?"

"Right. This guy was in the backyard. He wasn't bitten, but he was shot by mistake. He died there, and we didn't want you to think we did it."

"We only found two guys there—a guy with a gray beard, and a short balding guy," I said.

"Yeah—those are the guys who saved me. The guy in the yard had a skull tattoo on his forearm, and long brown hair," the man from house 644 said.

"Check number 644 again—there should be another body there," I said into the radio." I'm sorry, but I have to cover all my bases. Women over here with the children, and men over there. I need you to get naked," I said to the relieved father. I called the nurses and a guard into the locker room. The nurses looked over the kids and women, while the guard and I looked over the men. Everyone was clean. "I'm sorry for the trouble." They nodded in agreement.

"Logan, can you come to the lobby? Doc wants you," the guard radioed. I cut through the gym and went through the main door.

"What's up, Doc?" I said.

He pulled me outside. "Something's bugging me. How did this outbreak start?" I shrugged, afraid of the truth." Shawna was sick with what we thought was the flu, but what if we missed a wound?"

"Impossible. We checked them, and the bites are impossible to hide when you're naked."

"Exactly—or so I thought then. But this thing is like a virus. Like AIDS, you can get it by having a wound in your mouth and getting infected blood in there. Michelle said she killed her cousin up close and personal. She was fine before that. Maybe she got blood in her mouth."

"Or her eyes?" I offered.

"Shit—I hadn't thought of that. The thin membrane would have easily allowed the virus into the bloodstream."

"Keep this quiet," I said. "If it gets out they were the cause, those girls are as good as dead."

"I agree, but we don't know if that's even what started this. I'll cover up the body, if need be."

"Okay." By the time I got to the homes, it was almost 4 p. m. and they'd finished the eighth row.

"Any sign of the third body?" I asked Tristan.

"No—we checked often."

"We're down to two rows. We still have to go to ground zero—that's where most probably are." Like the previous two nights, we all crammed into the corner house—and like those nights, we woke up at 4:30. The sun wasn't up yet. I took a head count. One guy and a snowmobile were missing. I asked around and was told he went to relieve the watch and visibility got so bad that his partner didn't see him run away from his post. He wasn't sure how the he got away on a snowmobile, my guess was he pushed it and then started it when he was further away. I told everyone via radio about, Allen, the missing guard.

"I've got two figures up here by the distillery. We've got no defenses. I doubt they know we're here," the woman in the distillery said. I sent three guys on snowmobiles up there. Within an hour, they were back. The two figures were two poorly dressed elderly people. We started on the ninth row, and in the sixth house we found one room that had blood all over.

"Gym, I need everyone from house 913 inspected."

"You sure you can't do it?" Jade asked.

"Jade—can you do it? It'll take me longer to get there."

"And leave Simon's smelly ass? Sure thing," he said. We continued down the row, and two houses later, we came across a cat. I hadn't seen once in years, and it was scared of us. As I bent down to pet it, an arm reached out from the hallway and grabbed my wrist. I yelled, but my arm. was locked by a vice grip, I stumbled back, hitting my head on the floor. Then it was on me, its mouth wide open. A mixture of blood and saliva dripped onto my cheek—it had me pinned. I looked beyond it and saw a boy hitting it in the head. The body went limp on top of me.

"Wait!" I yelled and pushed it off of me. "Now!" He put a single bullet into its head. "If you get blood into your mouth, you can turn. Thanks, though."

"No problem. Did he get you?"

"Don't think so," I said as I started to strip.

"What are you doing?"

"These clothes are covered in its blood, and you need to inspect me." The boy looked me over and gave me a thumbs-up. I was perplexed. I went upstairs and found winter clothing two sizes too small. The dead man had a skull tattoo on his forearm, a bullet wound in his chest, and was bald. We'd found our third body." Gym—has Jade showed up yet?"

"No."

"Ask the people from 644 if the third guy had long brown hair?"

"Okay," the voice said. "Yep—with a skull tattoo on his arm," the voice said a minute later.

"Thanks."

"Jade's here."

"Give him the skinny. Take them to the locker room." About five minutes later, three shots were heard coming from the main road.

CHAPTER 11

"Shit—he's been shot," someone said, as if they accidentally pushed the transmit button.

"What happened?" I said. A minute passed, then another, and another. "Somebody tell me what the *fuck* is going on."

"Jade's been shot. He's walking it off. It hit him in the shoulder blade, and Doc says he'll be fine, but he'll have a stiff shoulder for a while. The other guy will be fine."

"What other guy?" I asked.

The man on the radio explained that as Jade approached a daughter and father, he could tell the daughter was sick and barely breathing. The dad had refused the nurses help. They were in a corner, and Jade asked if she was all right. He then spotted bloodstains on her tee-shirt, so he put his hand on his holster. Seeing this, the dad, a big dude, took a swing at Jade. Jade wasn't a small guy either, but the dad caught Jade as he reached up to block him. Just as Jade pushed the man back, another guy came from behind and hit Jade in the head. Jade stumbled and dropped to one knee, and in his anger he pulled out his gun and told the first guy to stand down. The second guy took a swing from behind again, but Jade moved slightly. Seeing his opportunity, the dad grabbed his daughter and started to run toward the front door. Jade shot the guy in the lower leg, and he fell on top of his dying daughter. That's when the second guy was joined by two others, and the three of them jumped Jade. A large crowd had gathered and Jade lost control of his gun and in the struggle it went off into his chest and just wide of him. The other guards grabbed the guy, his daughter and Jade. Once again, locking the doors behind them, they told the wounded man they were sorry and shot his six year old daughter out of sight from him.

"We've got to clear this place up," I said into the radio. "To combat cabin fever, let's have people get shovels and dig out paths to and from the gym, mess hall, and command center. Take as many volunteers as you want, and don't let anyone out of your sight. Tell them this way they can get out of the overcrowded gym. Do a head count twice before they go out and twice when they come in. If they see anything, tell them not to be a hero, just run away. Once the paths are done or it gets dark, send them in. Tomorrow do the same, but make a big one to the park by the command center. For the kids, hopefully it'll be over by then." I hoped this would cool down some of the people.

After the delay, we finished the ninth row and decided to call it a night, we were missing eighteen people, with the outbreak's ground zero the first place we'd go to re-count. I woke up at 3 a. m. in a cold sweat. I went to the window and saw the guys standing watch outside throwing snowballs. I went downstairs and opened the door and started to yell. I realized they couldn't be older than fifteen. The closest one to me dropped his snowball and walked away. "Just keep a lookout—be safe," I said to them. Despite my warning, the snow-balled armed one pelted the unarmed one in the back and they continued their fight. I went upstairs and looked out the window. The snow started picking up as the wind whipped it around, and I was beginning to lose sight of them. I opened the window, and yelled, "Get back inside—no sense in staying outside in this shit."

"I'm sorry about Jon," Buck said, scaring the shit out of me.

"I didn't even hear you. How long you been there?"

"A few minutes—I couldn't sleep either."

"Yeah, it's been a bad few days. I didn't realize you were part of this party."

"I started off as a wall watcher."

"Oh, that makes sense." We both stared out the window as the world was blanketed with white.

"Fresh snow is gonna make things rough," Buck said, breaking the silence.

"Yep." Deep down I knew it was going to be the worst day yet.

Buck paused to say, "At least we made it this far," then left.

By seven, the sun still hadn't broken through, and the cloudy sky was still dark. I scavenged up clothes while everyone slept. I let everyone sleep till 7:30, it was just light enough to see. We ate what little food was left. Not a word was said—call it dread or fatigue—but nobody wanted to clear that house.

"All right," I said. "We know that today is going to be bad. I don't want to go to that house, but we have to. We're going to that house first, and then start at the beginning of the row." Everyone grumbled. "We're all going to do that house. Groups of three check every nook and cranny. This house is just like the hundreds we've done." I was trying to motivate them.

"Except this one is full of dead people," a voice came from the back of the kitchen.

"Who should be dead, because Doc said he stabbed them," I replied.

"With a steak knife. They're still alive," a different voice said.

"Let's just set it on fire," the first voice said again.

"We can't," Tristan said.

"Why not?" someone asked.

"First, we need an exact count. Sixteen of eighteen unaccounted for should be in there. Besides, what if it spread? We don't exactly have a fire department," I said.

"So two are still out there?" someone said.

"We know Allen took off in the middle of the night. So make that seventeen in there. My bad," I said. We took off into the snowstorm, which was now blinding. The snow was close to three-and-a-half feet deep, and even our snowmobiles were struggling.

"The ice is breaking apart," Simon said cheerfully.

"Thanks. Any word on Jade?"

"Doc says he'll be fine, but he won't shut up about it. The people here are getting more restless—they don't want to shovel."

"We should be done by dinner." We got to the house, and the first thing we noticed was that there were several pairs of cold, dead eyes watching us through the front window. Whoever it was punched through the glass, and before I could say anything, the air was filled with the acrid odor of gunpowder. The dead fell out of sight.

"Maybe we *should* burn it down. I mean, seventeen is better than forty-eight," Tristan whispered in my ear.

I noticed he wasn't dressed as heavily as I was. "Aren't you cold?" I asked.

"Nah—I'm a real Midwesterner."

"Fair enough, but we need an exact count."

"All right—just saying. I'm sure these guys won't say anything."

"Yea but what if one escapes, turns more people? We'll be doing this again."

"Fine—just saying. We don't like the cold anymore than they do."

"I got it." He was pissing me off, so I turned to address the group. "Everyone—I know you're tired and cold. I am too, but we've come so far and we're almost done. Let's get it over with—then we can relax and drink hot chocolate with marshmallows. So surround the house, get about six feet from the person next to you. Fire no more than ten shots into the house, two M16s stay behind to spray the front."

Everyone took aim and fired. I'm sure everyone firing wasted more than ten shots, but it was better to be safe. The air now really smelled of burnt powder, but now there was a hint of decaying flesh. Nine guys went into through the back door, I went in the front with eight more. The two M16s stayed out by the snowmobiles. The living room was full of wounded dead. "Put one bullet in all of them," I said, but I was sure they were making extra sure. After fifteen minutes, we found and in some cases "killed" fifteen dead things. We all went back outside, I got the number added up from the gym, base, distillery, mess hall and jail. Still three short, I sent two men into the house to do a recount. Still three short. "Fuck!" I yelled. "Split up and search the remaining houses."

Three hours later, we were still missing three people. "I'm gonna check again, but I'm going alone. Wait outside." I wasn't checking. I saw Shawna's body—she been stabbed by Doc. Turns out a knife through the eye will do it. She was wearing sweatpants and a hoodie. Knowing I was on borrowed time, I looked all over and found a pair of surgical gloves. I took off her pants—no bites. It felt wrong, but I slid down her panties, and no bite marks. I covered her back up, then removed her hoodie. I was nervous that Shawna wasn't dead—well, dead, again. No bite marks anywhere. I moved her head toward a lamp and peered into her mouth. *This is where she comes back*, I thought. Still no movement. I could barely see inside, so I took the lampshade off. Low and behold—a patch of decaying flesh. She must have ingested some the bad blood. I put everything back as best I could, then went back outside, "We're still missing three, but I want these bodies burned. Bring them outside." I sent a couple of people back to warm up at the gym. Ten guys and I carried the bodies out. I made sure I got Shawna's body.

"That's weird," the kid helping me said.

"What is?" I asked.

"This girl doesn't have any blood on her."

"No—right there," I said, pointing at her eyes.

"Oh. Maybe Doc killed her by accident, thinking they got her."

"Maybe, but do me a favor—don't tell anyone," I said. "Doc's taking this pretty hard. He'd talked to these people daily. So he'd feel more guilty knowing one wasn't a zombie."

"Oh jeez—I hadn't thought about that. You're right. Doc would probably want to kill himself—and we need him."

"Yeah—we do. Thanks."

"No—thank you," the kid said.

Deep down I knew it might get out, but I knew Doc wouldn't say anything. If asked about it, I could always lie, but something was eating at me deep down. I had a feeling this would come back to haunt me. We burned the bodies, and the smell was just as bad as I remembered. Then we went to the mess hall. The women were already cooking, and the people from the gym were slowly making their way in. Once everyone was in, I grabbed the bullhorn because my voice was beyond hoarse. "I know we're all tired and just want to sleep in our beds. But there are still three people unaccounted for."

"Two—Allen came back. He had to find his daughter," a voice yelled from the back.

"Okay—there are still two out there. If they were bitten, then they've turned. We went to Jon's snowmobile and the path he took back, and there were twelve there. So I believe the missing two are at the south end of the island. My suggested plan is to let the snow melt and continue then." There were groans all around. "Hold on. You all can go home tonight and stay with enough food for a week. I need twenty additional volunteers. We're going to double up the patrols. The normal perimeter patrols will continue, but we'll use a new pattern of one, eight, seventeen, nine, ten, fifteen, and sixteen." I pointed at the map. "This way there will be at least five men or women to respond to any sightings at any given time, each house will have a flare gun. If you see something, then fire the flare. Does anyone see a problem with this? I cannot stress the issue enough. If you see something, don't be afraid to fire the flare. The rovers have those strobes on them, so don't mistake them for something else. Questions?"

"What about the new girls?" a woman asked.

"I believe they're innocent. Sure the timing is coincidental, but they too are grieving. Shawna was their sister and friend. Furthermore, they were inspected by some of you in this very room. So I ask you, did you see bite marks on any of them?" My eyes locked on the boy from earlier, and he shook his head. "No—and as far as I know, they didn't start this. I don't know how it started. Those things can walk under water—we experienced that two years ago—which is why we need to complete the wall. I believe deep down they

were just as innocent as anyone of us in here. Some of you
have talked with them—they were sex slaves to those men.
I moved them out to protect them. They're outsiders. I don't
blame you for thinking they had something to do with it. We
have two months of winter left, and this winter has been our
most difficult. This will be a trying year. The supplies on the
mainland are drying up. We've got tools and knowledge. We
can make this work because without each other. We're no
better than them. Any questions?"

One man raised his hand. "Who put you in charge?
Maybe I could run it better." It was Luke Johnson, a frequent
complainer.

"Maybe you could, but I like to think we've done a pretty
good job so far," I replied.

"Well, I think I could do better."

"But I've proven that this is working, so why change it?"

"Because I'm tired of you getting all the perks."

"What perks?"

"You don't know how good you have it."

"I guess not. Should we put this up to a vote?"

"Yes we should," he said, finally standing up.

"All right, if you think Luke here can do a better job than
me, please raise your hand—this is a democracy." All across
the room there was a total of six hands.

"Well, the people have spoken," he said as he stormed out
of the mess hall.

"I want all of you to know that if I ever falter or you think
you or someone else can do a better job than me, so be it. We
can put it to a vote. In fact, just so I don't have all this 'power,
' I say we form a council. List four people you think would
be strong, and the top ten names will form a council—and
each member will head a committee. Together we can make
this a better island. Bring the list in four days. I'm going to
talk to the outsiders." I drove over to the jail and told the jail-
ers to leave, they went to join their families, and I had the
girls alone.

"About time you got here," Michelle said.

"Don't fucking start with me." The girls all stiffened up. "What I'm about to tell you stays here. Don't breathe a word to anyone, because if you do, this island will turn on the six of us. Who knew she was infected?"

They all stared at me. Then Natasha said, "You made her strip."

"Yeah. The inside of her mouth was filled with pus. I think she got bad blood inside her mouth."

"From my cousin?" Michelle said.

"Yes. When she was hitting her, she must have gotten splatter in her mouth."

"Oh my God—we all got splattered because she came out of nowhere," Natasha said.

"Well, as far as I know, she was a victim," I said. They all nodded. I opened the door and led them to the snowmobile. I went back in to turn off the lights, and when I got back outside they were gone. I'd left my radio on the snowmobile so, too tired to think, I went back inside, closed my eyes, and drifted off to sleep. Moments later—or so it seemed—I was awakened by pounding on the door. It was the girls, and I was so pissed. "Not funny."

"We only went to the back side of the jail, and you went right back in. We've been pounding for like two hours, it was Alaina's idea," Nikki said.

"It was not," Alaina said, turning bright red.

"Man, that was a great nap," I said. I went home in the dark after taking the girls home. A lot of lights were on, Thank God the generators ran themselves. I barely had my shoes off when I passed out from pure exhaustion. I was awakened by an announcement coming over the PA about a memorial service at 11 a.m. at the chapel. "All are welcome as we pay our respects to all the people who had been lost." It was 9 a.m., the first time I'd gotten over five hours of sleep in weeks. I got to the chapel at 10:15 and asked the woman in charge if she needed help. She declined my offer and said I'd done enough.

The service had quite a turnout—probably everyone who wasn't patrolling was there. We had a few pictures of the fallen, and family members or friends said a few words. We broke for lunch at two p. m. It was one of those bright days that hurt your eyes if you weren't wearing sunglasses. After three days, there was no sign of the missing people. Allen and the wounded man were forgiven by all—well, all except Jade, who was still pissed. The list of nominees was finally collected and Michelle, Nikki, and I counted up the votes in command center. I hadn't really left there, other than the memorial or other random small trips, because I hoped to find the missing zombies. The top ten were selected, and based on the needs, they were named to head the island's various vital departments. The list:

Me—Mayor
Jade Griffith—Vice President
Doc—Medical Department
Anita Blackwell—Recreation and Education (she was a former teacher)
Joe Pingel—Maintenance
Alex Johnston—Supplies
Tristan Fox—Island Defense
Michael Anderson—Farming (obviously he was a former farm)
Gary Powers—Armory
Nicole Granderson—Home Owners
Liz Powers—Mess Hall

About two days later, the results were posted. We met the next day in the command center.

"You look like shit," Jade said to me, pulling up a chair.

"I wouldn't talk," I said.

"When was the last time you slept?"

"Last night."

"Where?"

"On the cot over there," I said, pointing to the back office.

"Eek," he said, making a face at me. Once everyone showed up, we had a meet-and-greet, and each person got their respective assignments. For the most part, they were pleased. I said, "I trust your judgment, all of you, so don't abuse this. We all need to give a little and give our fair share. That being said, if anyone on this council feels someone is abusing this privilege, they can recommend you be replaced. Then we'll vote anonymously to relieve you. All right—I need the following things from Alex—the supplies everyone needs. and where to get them. Joe, we need a way to get the snow cleared. The rest of you get Alex a list of supplies you need. Sorry Alex—you have a doozy of a job. If you need an assistant, pick someone you can trust. But get an inventory of what we have. If there are no questions, then I guess that's it."

Alex hung back. "Why me?" she asked.

"You're the best for the job. It gets you out of roving for awhile."

"I guess that's a plus." We broke up, and I went back to the cot.

CHAPTER 12

A week passed, and then another. The snow started to melt, and the island was trying to get back to normal as best it could. But there was still no sign of the missing two. We even checked the dilapidated sewer system. By the time all the snow melted, we'd given up hope that we'd find the two on the island. I finally moved back into my house, but it didn't feel right, so I packed up what little I had and moved a bed into the back office of the command center. I had officially become obsessed with the survival of this place.

After another two weeks, most of the people were relaxed and, I was finally starting to lower my guard around the island, Jade was back to full strength. Spring was almost upon us, the time of year to start planning. We brought the council into our meeting, we were way ahead of the two previous years, mainly because we made the decisions. The first run was slated for the first week of April, we were going to steal the cows and chickens Jon had seen by the airport.

"The ground is soft now," I said to Joe.

"I thought we were gonna start next week," Joe said.

"How far do you think we can get?"

"By end of fall, we can get through the remainder of the island. And I propose that if there's time, we can shore up the old wall." Joe sounded sure of himself.

"You really think so?" I asked, surprised.

"Probably. Okay, probably not," he confessed.

"Huh?"

"I don't have a clue about how to build a wall. I can fix engines and shit, but you need a builder."

"Okay—find someone to supervise." The meeting ended after two hours. I was walking out with Jade and he lit up a cigarette. "Where do you keep getting those?" I asked.

"Don't worry about it. Hey—you've got a visitor," he said, pointing at Michelle.

"Hey," I said, surprised to see her.

"Hey you," she said, coming over to kiss me.

"What was that for?" I said.

"Don't worry about it. Follow me," she said. We started walking along our usual path. "So what are we going to do?"

"Do?" I asked curiously.

"Us, this—you."

"Me? What do you mean?"

"Don't be a retard. I've been throwing myself at you."

"Well I've been busy, in case you hadn't noticed."

"I know, but you need a release from the world." With that, she leaned in and kissed me again. "I'm ready for you," she said, smiling. And then we headed back to the command center. Where she pushed me onto my bed.

Afterwards, we held each other and talked about our future, and we decided that in this crazy world we needed each other. We continued on like this for several weeks.

At a subsequent meetings, we determined that we'd make one run for the cattle and chickens and another two runs for all the medical, food, and miscellaneous things we needed. We actually planned routes months in advanced so we could be prepared for anything that was out in the wild, wild west of the mainland.

The first run was a week away, and spring was in full swing. Our walks continued, but Michelle was starting to feel queasy and wasn't eating. She went to see Doc and came back full of smiles.

"Guess who?" she said, putting her hands over my eyes.

"Taking those big, rough hands into account, it must be Jade."

"Ass. No—try the mother of your child."

"What?" I said, turning around.

"Know how I was getting sick? Well, Doc made me pee on a stick, and guess what it said."

"Obviously, it said you weren't. Thank God."

"What? You aren't excited?"

"Of course I am. I'm teasing you."

"You'd better be, because guess what?"

"What?"

"I love you," she said.

"Well, I love you too."

"Do you really?" she asked, blushing.

"Of course—why wouldn't I?"

"I don't know—I'm a girl."

"Oh, stop. You're the woman I love, carrying my child."

"Good."

We were now planning a future with a baby in it. The next five days passed in the blink of an eye. On the day before our first run, Michelle came up to the back office, now without a bed. I had moved with Michelle to a different house, since I was no longer a single guy. "Guess what we need to do tonight?" she asked.

"Sex?"

"Ha-ha. Of course, but something else."

"What? I'm not trying to be mean, but we're going on a raid tomorrow, Sweetie. So could you just tell me?" I said.

"Sorry—I'm such a pain."

"Stop it. What is it?"

"Well, the wall is almost finished along the north end of the island. I figured it'd be a romantic way to spend a few hours before you go. You know—in case something happens tomorrow? It would be nice to see the water not be obstructed by a wall."

"I guess I can spare a few minutes," I said, offering my hand.

"Thanks," she said. I noticed her eyes were tearing up.

"Is everything okay?" I asked, looking down.

"Oh, it's nothing—I'm just being stupid."

"No—tell me."

"Well, we haven't even talked about the baby, and what if something happens to you? How am I supposed to live without you?"

"I love you and I give you my word that tomorrow after the raid I'll be here and we'll watch the sun set, like we are now."

"Okay." We stopped walking and started watching the sun dance across the river as it set, making the sky around it and the water a brilliant shade of orange and pink.

"Contact!" my radio screamed at me, followed by several shots. It was Jade. I looked at her, she looked at me, and her eyes pleaded for me to stay.

"Where at?" I asked. grabbing her hand and kissing it. She smiled at me.

"North shore, and it ain't a zombie—they're firing at me!" his panicked voice said. She let go of my hand.

"Go. Obviously it's bad," she said.

"No—we go back to command center. I'm a father now." She let out a little laugh. "What is it?" I asked the radio.

"They're on a flat bed—they're doing something. I can't tell what," Jade said.

"Incoming." It was Simon now. That's when we heard it— four quick thuds followed by a whistling sound overhead. Four explosions rocked the ground behind us.

"Run!" I yelled to her. We took off running toward the command center.

"They're out of range—I can't hit them. Second wave incoming!" Simon yelled over the radio. Four more quick thuds followed another whistling sound overhead. There was an explosion fifteen feet in front of us. Michelle stopped running and turned to look at me, and before I could say anything, another explosion hit right behind her.

CHAPTER 13

"Ugh," I said as I tried to raise my head. I looked down and I was strapped in what looked like a hospital bed.

"He's waking up," Alaina said as Doc came over.

"How you feeling?" He asked. "Go get Jade," he whispered to her.

"Where am I? What happened? Why am I strapped down?" I asked

"A lot has happened, so just remain calm," Doc said.

"Calm? I'm strapped down, why wouldn't I be calm?"

"Because you socked me pretty good," Jade said wearing a nice shiner.

"Where is Michelle? Release me." I demanded.

"We can't do that," Jade said.

"What happened?"

"We will tell you but you have to remain calm," Doc said.

"I swear if one more person, tells me to remain calm, I'll snap."

"Fine, you want to know what happened?" Jade said, sitting on the bed.

"Hell yes."

"She's gone. You've been in and out of consciousness for the past two weeks; this is the second time we told you about what happened. The first time you snapped and tried to get away. You caught me off-guard and Doc put you back under," Jade explained.

"What do you mean gone? I just saw her along the waterfront," I stopped remembering the last few images I saw. I welled up remembering the explosion that rocked just behind her. "But she was right in front of me?"

"I can't say for sure but when we found you guys, she was on top of you. I think had she not been in front of you, you'd be dead. And quite frankly, you should be dead. It took us about five hours to find you and you lost a lot of blood," Jade said.

"I wish I was dead."

"They share your pain," Doc said as he moved my curtains. The room had at least 8 other beds full of people, each in various stages of wounds.

"What happened?" I asked Jade.

"The mainlanders used mortars on us," Jade said seriously.